The Eden Stories

The Longest Day

Terry Toler

The Longest Day

Published by: BeHoldings, LLC.
Copyright @2020, **BeHoldings, LLC**
Terrytoler.com.
All Rights Reserved

Unless otherwise noted, all Scripture quotations are taken from the Holy Bible, New Living Translation, copyright © 1996, 2004, 2015 by Tyndale House Foundation. Used by permission of Tyndale House Publishers, Inc., Carol Stream, Illinois 60188. All rights reserved.

Cover and interior designs: BeHoldings, LLC.
Editor: Jeanne Leach.

Our books can be purchased in bulk for promotional, educational and business use. Please contact your bookseller or the BeHoldings Publishing Sales department at: sales@terrytoler.com

For booking information email: booking@terrytoler.com:

First U.S. Edition: October 2020
Printed in the United States of America

ISBN 978-1-7352243-0-5

This is a work of fiction. All of the characters, organizations, and events portrayed in this novel are either products of the author's imagination or are used fictitiously. Any resemblance to actual persons, living or dead is entirely coincidental.

BOOKS BY TERRY TOLER

Fiction

The Longest Day
The Reformation of Mars
The Great Wall of Ven-Us
Saturn: The Eden Experiment
The Late, Great Planet Jupiter
Save The Girls
The Ingenue
The Blue Rose
Saving Sara
Save The Queen
No Girl Left Behind
The Launch
Body Count
Mercury Protocols

Non-Fiction

How to Make More Than a Million Dollars
The Heart Attacked
Seven Years of Promise
Mission Possible
Marriage Made in Heaven
21 Days to Physical Healing
21 Days to Spiritual Fitness
21 Days to Divine Health
21 Days to a Great Marriage
21 Days to Financial Freedom
21 Days to Sharing Your Faith
21 Days to Mission Possible
7 Days to Emotional Freedom
Uncommon Finances
Uncommon Marriage
Uncommon Health
Suddenly Free
Feeling Free

For more information on these books and other resources
visit TerryToler.com.

PRAISE FOR THE TERRY TOLER NOVELS

"Terry Toler books are so riveting!"

"When you think you've got the plot worked out, he puts a twist on it and surprises you."

"I couldn't put them down and kept reading one after another."

"Never a dull moment in a Terry Toler novel."

"I love them. Every book has plenty of action and conflict."

"Terry Toler is my new favorite author."

"I love the new style of writing he has invented."

"Not everyone can write an ending like Terry Toler."

"Great writing style! Every novel captures me at the first chapter and then I can't put them down."

"I love all the twists and turns."

"I don't even like fiction, but I love your books."

"You really know how to draw an audience into your story, and I am a perfect example of that."

"I have to force myself to quit reading, so I can get some work done."

"Every time I finish a chapter, I say it's going to be my last, and the intrigue doesn't let me. I have to keep reading one more chapter!"

"Your cliffhangers are epic."

"I recognize a Terry Toler book from the first paragraph."

"Your books have it all. Romance. Intrigue. Mystery. Suspense. And endings that make you come back for more."

"I'm hooked on Terry Toler books."

"The Eden Stories are revolutionary. You've created your own new genre of fiction."

"Wow! That's all I can say."

"When I finish a book, I think about it for days which is the characteristic of a great author."

"I can't wait to see what you come up with next."

"I love the characters. They draw me in, and I find myself rooting for them."

PART ONE

The greatest explorer on this earth never takes voyages as long as those of the man, who descends to the depth of his heart.
- Julien Green.

Chapter One

Today was Adam Lang's last day on earth.

Most people don't know when their last day will be; Adam had known for more than two years. He stared at himself in the mirror, looking for any sign of emotion. Nothing. His ex-wife, may she rest in peace, said he was dead inside. The Process Communication Model concluded that Adam was a thinker, not a feeler. The more in-depth tests said he "has a penchant for solitude and a low need for affiliation." His third-grade teacher was ahead of the curve when she wrote on his report card, *doesn't play well with others.*

Adam turned his head to see if he had missed any spots shaving. "I need to talk to Jamie," he said to himself.

Another special report from the television in the other room interrupted his thoughts. The big four networks and all the cable news channels had been talking about him almost nonstop for two straight hours.

Maybe Jamie is watching the news.

If she was, she wouldn't know he was her father. He wanted nothing more than to tell her, but would she want to know?

A loud knock on the door startled him. "Open up, Lang."

He found the remote to silence the television.

The banging on the door got louder. Adam didn't need to look at the clock to know the time. His handler, Rod Grisham, said he'd pick Adam up at eight, and in twelve years, he'd never been one minute early or one minute late. Sarge, as everyone called him, banged harder on the door, not giving Adam a second to answer. If anyone at the hotel was asleep, they weren't anymore. Sarge didn't care. He thought if anyone was asleep at eight o'clock in the morning, they were a loser, and someone should wake them up.

"I'm coming, Sarge. Hang on."

"Are you ready, Lang?"

"I'm not going."

"You *are* going. If I have to drag you there myself."

"You and whose army?" Adam said with caution, and he'd soon know if Sarge was in the mood to joke around.

Sarge stood five feet ten and was two-hundred pounds of solid muscle. If he wanted to drag Adam out of there, he could easily do it. "The three of us. Me, myself, and I are the only army I need to haul you skinny, little, runt out of this room and down to the car."

"Seriously, Sarge, I'm not going."

"They thought you might say that. That's why they sent me."

"I need to talk to Jamie."

"That's ridiculous. It's too late now."

"She needs to know that I'm her father."

"What are you going to say? 'Hi Jamie. I'm your father. By the way, you're never going to see me again. Watch the news. They'll tell you why.'"

"Don't you think a girl should know who her father is?" Adam asked. He'd never get another chance and had been thinking of Jamie for months now—ever since his ex-wife died and he found out he'd been a father all these years.

Why didn't Andrea want me to know?

"The poor girl already lost her mother. She doesn't even know you exist. She already lost you once; do you want her to lose you again?" Sarge grabbed a piece of toast off of the mostly uneaten breakfast tray. "You should eat something. It's going to be a long day."

Sarge's phone rang. He answered it.

Adam said, "Tell her I'm not going to do it."

"We're leaving right now," Sarge told the person on the other end. Most likely Sarah. "Our ETA should be in twenty minutes. Yeah, he's doing okay. Are you sure you want to put him on television? His face is better suited for radio, don't you think?"

Adam was not amused. "Tell her I'm not going to do it."

Sarge ignored him. "We'll be there." He hung up the phone and shoved it back into his pocket.

"What did she say?" He couldn't really do anything if Sarah Reynolds, flight director for NASA, told him to go to the press conference. She was both of their bosses.

"We have to be at Kennedy in thirty minutes. She said to not let you sneak out the back and to keep my eyes on you at all times. She also said she thinks she made a mistake picking you, but it's too late now. Let's roll. You have a flight to catch." He faced Adam squarely. "She also said to make sure you look pretty for the cameras."

Adam groaned.

"What's the big deal? You're ready for it."

That was true. For the past two weeks, a PR expert had been working with Adam on how to answer questions from the press. They ran through mock sessions and grilled him for forty minutes straight several times a day until he got it right. All the answers were scripted. He only had to memorize them and spit them out at the right time, which he could do in his sleep.

Still, the thought of speaking in front of a crowd terrified him. "If it's so easy," he said, "you do it. You know I don't like attention, and you know I don't like speaking in front of a crowd."

"Don't be such a pansy. There's not a crowd. Only about a hundred reporters will be in the room. Two hundred million people will be watching, but don't pay any attention to that. If you get flustered, look over at me and picture me in my underwear. That should get your mind off of the crowd."

Sarge almost smiled for a change.

"I don't think me throwing up in front of two hundred million people will help anything."

"Then pick out a pretty reporter and picture her in her underwear. Whatever works for you. You're doing this," he stated. "Let's go and get this over with."

Sarge had his marching orders, so he took charge as only he could do. "Here's the drill. There's a motorcade waiting in the underground garage. We'll have a police escort that'll take us to Kennedy. Senator Robinson will ride with you, and I'll be in the car behind you. There will be more than two-hundred-thousand people lining the route, so smile and wave. You're a frigging rock star now. Don't let it go to your head."

Sarge walked over and grabbed Adam's suitcase. As they were about to leave, Sarge stopped and pulled Adam into a bear hug—an act out of character for Sarge. He caught Adam off guard, and it took him a moment to hug him back.

Sarge looked at Adam and said, "I'm going to miss your sorry self." The only time Sarge had ever touched him other than a handshake was when Adam jokingly challenged him to a wrestling match. That was a mistake. Sarge put him in a bear hug, slammed him to the ground, and choked him out in less than a minute. He wanted to teach Adam a lesson so he held the chokehold longer than he should have.

It worked. Adam never messed with Sarge again.

"If you start crying, I'm not going with you," Adam said. "You probably want to borrow some money from me, because you know I won't be able to collect it after today. You'll miss me for about five minutes, then you'll be on somebody else's case, and you'll have forgotten my name."

Sarge headed for the door.

I really am going to miss Sarge.

He was going to miss Jamie too. She would miss him as well, if she knew who he was.

Adam resigned himself to the probability he was never going to talk to Jamie. He didn't even know how to get in touch with her. So, he turned his mind to the monumental task at hand. This was his fifteen minutes of fame he never asked for, but he figured it'll be easy.

How hard could it be? I answer a few questions. Twenty minutes tops. Then I'm out of there and I can focus on my mission.

He'd always wanted to be an astronaut, and today would be his defining moment... the culmination of years of preparation and training.

The first man to go to the end of the universe.

* * *

Jamie Austen had been looking for her father for two years. She spent the past two hours of her spring break sitting on the edge of her bed at the Beach Street Resort in Miami Beach, listening intently to them talk about him nonstop on the television.

She googled Cape Canaveral on her phone and discovered she was only four hours away from there. The news said her father's launch was in six hours. Could she make it in time? And if she did, how would she get past security?

"Would he even talk to me?" she asked aloud, "He doesn't even know I exist, so of course they wouldn't let me through."

Doesn't a man have a right to know he has a daughter?

She stood and paced the room. "I have to try. I promised."

Tears welled up in Jamie's eyes. She remembered sitting on her mother's deathbed.

"I have something important to tell you," Mom told her in earnest. "Will you ever be able to forgive me?"

"What, Mom? Of course, I forgive you. What is it?"

The secret she had held deep inside of her for seventeen years came pouring out. More of a confession than anything else. The guilt, the betrayal, the lies. All Jamie's life, her mother had told her that her father was dead. She now needed to make things right.

"He was a really good man. He was the love of my life. I was jealous of his career and was afraid I'd be left a widow and you without a father. I didn't think I could take a husband who was an astronaut. What if he died a horrible death in space? I couldn't stand the thought. I couldn't put you through it."

Jamie remembered her mom's anguish like it was yesterday.

"I never told him about you. He deserved to know. I was wrong. He never even knew I was pregnant."

So, she had lost him under her own terms, and Jamie had grown up without a father anyway.

Her mother confessed she'd made a horrible mistake. It wasn't fair to Jamie or her father.

"Please find him. Tell him I'm sorry. I was wrong. Tell him I've always loved him." Her mother gripped her hand. "Jamie, you need to know your father. His name is Adam Lang. You are just like him. With me gone... you're going to need him."

Then she died.

Jamie was seventeen back then. She went to live with her aunt and then went to college. Every chance she got; Jamie searched. There was no Adam Lang on social media. How could she know he was locked away in a training program for the last two years? All her calls to NASA were not returned.

She now knew where he was. He was four hours away. This was her last chance. The news said he was about to leave on a mission to the ends of the universe and would never return.

"What am I going to say? 'Hi Dad. I'm your daughter. I know you're never going to see me again. Sorry.'"

The words didn't make sense. They didn't have to. She had to keep her promise to her dying mother. She had to do it for herself. She needed to talk to him, if only for a minute.

Jamie quickly scribbled a note to her roommate, grabbed her purse and keys, and headed for the lobby. She hadn't eaten, so she stopped by the gift shop in the lobby. She purchased two bottles of water, a Met RX protein bar, a package of gum, and a tee shirt that said, *Life Would Be Boring Without Me.* The tee shirt was a present for her dad. Something he could take with him on his trip. Something to remember her by.

As Jamie exited the store, she saw the guy who had been randomly appearing everywhere she went. An employee at the hotel. He was at the beach the day before when she was sunbathing. She caught him gawking at her from a distance. Then in the bar later that night while she and her friends were dancing, he even came up to her and asked if he could buy her a drink. She told him she didn't drink, which wasn't a lie, but she wouldn't have accepted a drink from him anyway. She didn't trust him to not put something in her drink. He wouldn't leave her alone and asked her to dance.

She said no a little more rudely and made up an excuse, saying she had a boyfriend and she wasn't interested. He stormed away like he was offended. The guy gave her the creeps. Now, he was in the lobby. It looked like he was there waiting for her.

It didn't matter. Soon, she'd be hundreds of miles away.

Jamie quickly walked to the elevator to the parking garage. He started to follow her, but she gave him a nasty, "leave me alone, not interested" kind of look, and he turned away. She breathed a sigh of relief when he didn't get on the elevator with her.

Oh well. I'm probably just imagining things anyway.

She turned her focus to the task at hand—getting to Cape Canaveral as soon as possible. Jamie pushed the button for level two and thought about what she was going to say if and when she talked to her father for the first time.

She exited the elevator and walked toward her car and sensed movement behind her to her right.

The man from the lobby.

Her instinct was right.

He had been stalking her.

Chapter Two

9:00 a.m. Six hours to launch.

When Courtney Dixon first met Adam, their relationship was strictly professional. Now she was in love with him. *How could I have let this happen?* NASA had strict rules about dating an astronaut. Technically, they had never dated. *But still...*

They had just finished their phone call, and she had wished him luck at his press conference. He didn't seem nervous. Adam was solid as a rock under pressure. That was also the reason NASA chose him for the mission. He never let anyone know what he was feeling, except her. All kinds of thoughts and emotions flooded into her head. After Adam left her house about nine-thirty the night before, she had cried herself to sleep.

Courtney turned on the television in her living room as the press conference was starting. Adam walked out wearing his NASA jacket and looked the part. The crowd gave him a standing ovation. He took a seat in front of a large wall with the universe as the backdrop and a picture of his spacecraft, Chronos 7, flying off into space.

The Administrator of NASA, John Matthews spoke first. Two other men were on the panel. Senator Joe Robinson, the driving force behind getting the funding through Congress, and Jake Laughton, CEO of Boeing, who designed the spacecraft.

Courtney thought back to the first time she met Adam at the employee cafeteria.

"Hello, Adam. My name is Courtney. Do you mind if I join you?"

He looked up from a book he was reading and said, "Sure. Suit yourself."

Courtney sat down across from him.

"I know you," Adam said. "You're a psychologist here at NASA. I hate psychologists. No offense." One thing about Adam. He didn't always say how he felt, but he always said what he was thinking.

"No offense taken... I guess. I saw you from across the room, and I wanted to meet you. I'm fascinated by your mission. Yes, I'm one of the space psychologists here at NASA." She was part of a team of psychologists whose jobs were to evaluate the mental and emotional health of the astronauts to see if they were fit for the rigors of space travel.

Adam was not assigned to her, but he was the talk of the office. He had the highest IQ ever recorded by an astronaut—195—and the lowest score of any astronaut on emotional intelligence.

Fascinating.

"Did they send you here to give me more tests?" he asked. "I hate taking those personality tests."

"I know. I read your file. And no, they didn't send me here to talk to you. I'm just curious."

"Curious about what?"

"Curious as to what would possess a man to leave everything on earth to spend a thousand years alone in space."

Courtney's thoughts were interrupted by the first question directed toward Adam.

"Why is the mission called The Longest Day?"

"When you travel at the speed of light," Adam answered, "your body doesn't age. Even though I'll be on the spacecraft for a thousand years, I'll only age one day. This is literally going to be the longest day of my life."

The room roared in laughter.

"This question is for Administrator Matthews. Why did you choose Adam for this mission?"

"Adam was one of the most qualified candidates in the history of NASA. He's highly educated and intelligent. He's also an extremely hard worker. I can't tell you how many hours he dedicated to preparing for this mission. He also spent time on the International Space Station, so he has had experience in space. That was critical. He went there twice. We wanted someone who knew what to expect and could adapt well to a weightless environment. Adam has a stellar record. As you can imagine, this is a unique mission. We were looking for a specific personality type, and Adam fit it perfectly. Adam has an incredible amount of courage, and we are extremely proud of him."

Courtney laughed to herself. The Administrator said Adam had the right personality. He'd passed that part of the evaluation by the skin of his teeth. Adam had been very uncooperative with her colleagues. She remembered asking him about the tests.

"Why do you hate taking the personality tests so much?"

"I think they're a waste of time. Ability and intelligence are more important than feelings."

"On one test, you answered every question, 'None of your business.'"

Adam laughed. "I know. I'm lucky I even got this job. Did you see the results from my Rorschach test?"

"I did. Why did you answer that every ink blot on every card looked like a rabbit?"

"I just thought it would be funny."

"The interviewer didn't think it was funny. He wasn't very kind in his evaluation. We use those tests to determine if someone has the personality to be an astronaut. It could have cost you your position on this mission."

The psychologist's recommendations held a lot of weight. Adam was so head and shoulders above everyone else, they let it slide.

Adam just shrugged. He leaned in and whispered, "Do you want to know why I said that each card looked like a rabbit."

Courtney listened intently.

"Because I'm hare-brained."

"You're mocking me."

"No. I'm not mocking you. I'm sorry. I thought that was funny."

It was funny. He's funny, witty, charming... and cute.

Courtney instinctively turned her attention back to the television set. A pretty reporter had stepped to the podium.

"My name is Alicia Cook with USA Today. Commander Lang, how are you feeling knowing that you are leaving everything behind, and you will never be coming back to earth again?"

Courtney chuckled. "He probably just wants to say, 'I have no feelings. Next question.'"

"I have mixed emotions," Adam said. "I'm sad to leave all of you good people behind and all my dear friends at NASA, but I'm also excited and extremely honored to have been chosen for this adventure. I just hope that I can make my country and the entire planet proud."

Another reporter stood. "My name is Bob Michaels, and I'm with the BBC. Where will your mission take you?"

"My destination is Kepler 452b. It's the farthest known spot in the universe. We know the universe is flat. It takes fourteen-hundred years to get there at the speed of light, but because I'll be traveling faster than the speed of light, I'll get there in a thousand years. I'm literally going to the edge of the universe as we know it. Kepler is the one planet in the universe that is most like earth. I'm hoping to find life on Kepler."

Another reporter took her turn. "Olivia York. Washington Post. Can a person survive traveling at the speed of light?"

"I'll find out in a few hours," Adam said.

The room got somber.

Adam continued. "Einstein proved in the theory of relativity that man can't survive traveling at the speed of light. However, we discovered that the universe was expanding faster than the speed of light, and it has a space stream not unlike the jet stream here on earth. When I enter the space stream, I'll be traveling at the same speed the universe is expanding. The earth is traveling at 67,000 miles an hour right now around the sun. We don't even notice it. If I'm attached to the stream, our belief is that I won't notice how fast I am going."

"How will we know if you survive entrance into the space stream?" the reporter asked.

"You won't," Adam answered soberly. "About one hour after launch, I'll enter the stream and will accelerate to a speed faster than the speed of light. We have no idea if my body can withstand that speed. If I survive, I'll send back a signal, but I'll be so far away from earth it'll take a hundred years to get back here. Everyone in this room will be gone by then."

Courtney shuddered.

That was the hardest part. Not knowing. Once Adam left, she wouldn't know if he lived or died. Adam assured her he'd done the calculations and would probably survive. *Probably?* That wasn't good enough. She'd have to live with not knowing for the rest of her life. She muted the television. She couldn't listen anymore.

* * *

Jamie quickened her steps to avoid a confrontation with her stalker. Time was of the essence, and she had to get to her dad before it was too late. She reached into her purse and felt for the can of mace in the bottom, but didn't think she'd need it, so she took her hand back out.

When she got to her car, she turned and faced him. He looked her up and down. He tried to look confident, like he'd done this before, but Jamie wasn't buying it. He was an employee of the hotel, and he still wore his name tag.

She chuckled to herself, "Who attacks a woman in broad daylight while wearing a name tag?"

Focus Jay. You don't have time for this. You must get to Cape Canaveral. Get rid of this joker as soon as possible.

"Fletcher, you don't want to do this," she said firmly.

Fletcher had a puzzled look on his face, obviously wondering how she knew his name.

She motioned with her eyes to his chest.

He pulled off the name tag and put it in his left pocket. His right hand was in his right pocket.

He must feel awfully stupid. He is stupid.

"Like I said, Fletcher, you need to turn and walk away while you still can." Jamie said it nicely, hoping he'd leave.

"And why would I do that?" he asked sarcastically.

"Because if you don't, you'll be eating your food through a straw for the next six months."

Fletcher was obviously holding a weapon in his right pocket, or at least he wanted her to think he was. Jamie hoped it wasn't a gun because that would complicate things.

Fletcher clumsily pulled it out; it was a knife, and on the second try he got it to open. The knife was in his right hand which meant that he was right-handed, but his weight was shifted slightly on his back, left foot which meant he was totally out of balance. He obviously had no clue what he was doing.

Jamie could easily outrun him, and that's what she would've done, but she didn't have time. She needed to get into her car and get going. Her self-defense instructor always said flight was better than fight. This time she didn't have the luxury of flight because every second mattered. Maybe she could talk some sense into him.

She stepped away from the car, trying to seem less threatening but mainly to improve her angle. Geometry and angles were her passion. When in a dangerous situation, angles are paramount. Not that she considered this a dangerous situation. He had a knife, but it was clear he didn't know how to use it. Nevertheless, anyone with a knife who weighed three hundred pounds had to be taken somewhat seriously.

She wanted to control the situation and defuse it if possible, "Fletcher, you have a choice. You should turn around, walk away, and we'll forget this ever happened. You're messing with the wrong girl. I know how to kill you with my bare hands in a hundred different ways."

Fletcher paused.

"Make the right choice here, Fletcher. You don't want to do this." Jamie used his name to make it personal so he would walk away. She then realized knowing his name complicated things. He might have walked away, but she could identify him. She knew his name and where he worked. He was probably thinking she'd turn him in, and he'd lose his job. That changed the dynamics. He probably wasn't going to walk away; he had to make sure she couldn't identify him.

Fletcher shifted his weight to the right and then back again to the left—a sign he was thinking about making his move. He wasn't going to back down.

She had challenged his manhood and he was regaining his courage. Jamie put her purse on top of the car and sat her bag with the water and power bar on the ground. She needed to have her hands free. Taking two steps toward Fletcher, she took him by surprise.

The closer she stood to him the less room he had to swing wildly and perhaps nick her with his knife. The body contained several arteries that could cause one to bleed out even if only slightly nicked, and she wasn't going to take any chances. Plus, her instructor always said, *Always make your first move a surprise. Throw your attacker off guard. Get him off his plan right away.*

Fletcher shifted his weight forward, telegraphing he was about to swing the knife toward Jamie's head. That made him even more unbalanced. He was slower than she imagined. Instead of a swing, he merely waved the knife at her.

Jamie attacked the knife with both hands, simultaneously striking his wrist with her right hand and the back of his hand with her left, knocking the knife out of his hands. The knife slid a good twenty feet away. An experienced fighter might have been ready for what was a common maneuver.

Fletcher barely reacted. He let out a groan and winced from the pain.

She'd hit him harder than she intended, and his wrist probably had some soft tissue damage he'd feel for a while. Jamie could have finished him at that moment, but she didn't want to hurt him so badly she'd have to call the police then wait for an ambulance and maybe even have to go to the station to make a statement. She didn't have time for that and had to leave immediately if she was going to make it to the launch in time.

Now that he was disarmed, she took several steps backward hoping he would run away. Unfortunately, she forgot about the bag on the ground. She stepped on the bottled water and fell flat on her back. With nothing to brace her fall, her head hit the pavement. For a moment, everything went black.

Emboldened, Fletcher pounced on top of her and grabbed her arms as he tried to use his superior weight to hold her down.

This is not good.

It didn't matter how inept this guy was, he weighed close to three hundred pounds, and he could do serious damage quickly if she didn't get out of the situation immediately.

Fletcher tried to hold her with one arm and hit her with the other.

Instinctively, she blocked most of them, but one clipped her in the ear causing her to see stars. She had to end this soon or she would be in trouble.

She remembered her training. Jamie lifted the right side of her hips causing Fletcher to lean to his right. At the same time, she freed her arm from his grip, grabbed his wrist, and twisted counter-clockwise while pulling violently downward, effectively separating his arm from his shoulder socket.

Fletcher cried out in pain.

Jamie placed her right hand under his right arm and jerked his elbow up while moving his wrist down. His arm hyperextended and tore all the cartilage and ligaments in his elbow. The bone in his arm snapped.

Fletcher's face twisted from fear and pain as he looked at his arm dangling helplessly from his shoulder.

In one fluid motion, Jamie brought her right elbow back toward Fletcher's head with incredible speed, connecting on Fletcher's cheekbone, shattering every bone on the right side of his face. She must have miscalculated her point of impact or his head was smaller than she realized because she caught part of his eye socket, breaking it as well.

Fletcher immediately collapsed with a moan.

Jamie pushed him off her and picked herself up off the pavement. She mentally scanned her body to see if anything hurt. The back of her head did, and she reached back and felt blood matting up in her hair. Nothing that would require stitches, but she'd have to stop and clean it, wasting even more time.

She picked up her bag, grabbed her purse, got in the car, and sped out of the garage. As she left, she looked around and didn't see any security cameras, which was a surprise considering this was a four-star resort.

With no cameras, it would be his word against hers, not that he would be able to talk anytime soon. Anyway, who would believe she attacked him? Florida had a stand your ground law and this was clearly self-defense. She would have to explain why she left the scene, which was problematic, but she would worry about that later. She had to get to Kennedy Space Center so her dad could help her sort it all out. She got her phone out of the purse and dialed 911.

"This is 911. What is your emergency?"

"A man is assaulting a woman on the second floor of the parking garage at the Beach Street hotel. There are injuries, so send an ambulance. When the EMTs arrive, tell them that the man has an orbital fracture and there may be hemorrhaging of the brain. Please hurry!"

"What is your name?"

Jamie hung up.

Chapter Three

9:40 a.m. Five hours, twenty minutes to launch.

T he press conference was going longer than had been anticipated. Courtney couldn't stop crying. Couldn't stop remembering...

"Do you want to come over to my house for dinner tomorrow night?" she'd asked Adam that day they met.

"Are you asking me on a date?" Adam said.

"No. It's not a date. I'm not allowed to date my subjects."

"So, I'm your subject now?"

"That's not what I mean. It's strictly professional. I just want to get to know what makes you tick. I'm a psychologist. You are the most interesting subject I have ever come across."

"You're right. That doesn't sound much like a date to me. I don't know how I feel about being one of your 'subjects.'"

They'd hit it off immediately. Adam was so easy to talk to, and Courtney's interest quickly turned from professional to a deep friendship. Somewhere along the line it turned to love. She remembered when.

"I have a date tonight," he said nonchalantly months later.

"What?" Courtney sat straight up in her chair. "Who do you have a date with?"

Stay cool. Don't let him see it bothers you. Why am I jealous?

"One of the astronauts set me up on a blind date."

"Really. Where are you taking her?" She tried not to sound too interested.

"I thought I'd take her to that French restaurant, *Amelie*."

"That's fancy. You must be trying to impress this girl."

"I don't even know her. It's the first date I've been on since my divorce. It may be a waste of money. I'm picking her up at six o'clock."

Her phone rang at seven thirty. It was Adam.

"Adam. Is something wrong? Aren't you supposed to be on your date?"

"Nothing's wrong. The date's over. I just dropped her off at her house. Can I come over?"

"Sure. Are you okay?"

"I'll tell you everything when I get there."

Courtney quickly straightened the house and changed out of her pajamas. She tossed an empty container of ice cream in the trash. Ice cream was her comfort food. The date had bothered her more than she was willing to admit to herself. Whatever had happened, the date hadn't gone well, and she was relieved.

How is Adam feeling? I was the first person he called.

Twenty minutes later, when Adam arrived at her house, he was clearly distressed. She had a glass of iced tea waiting for him. They went out on the back porch and sat on the swing. Adam looked out at the stars. Courtney wasn't sure if he was thinking about the mission or was still thinking about his date. Either way, she wanted to make him feel comfortable, relaxed, and make him feel like he could open up.

Don't rush it.

They sat in silence for the first minute or two. Adam obviously wasn't going to have an easy time sharing.

Curiosity was getting the best of her. Finally, Courtney broke the silence. "Tell me what's going on, Adam."

"Do you promise you won't laugh at me?"

"I promise. What happened?"

"Everything was going okay. We were having a pretty good conversation. She's a nice girl and kind of pretty. But..." His face grew serious.

"What?" Courtney said. "Just tell me what happened."

"She put salt on her food," Adam said with such intensity, he could have been talking about a murder the woman had just committed.

Courtney burst out laughing. His words didn't match the tone.

"You promised you wouldn't laugh."

She bit her lip and tried to compose herself. "I'm sorry. I don't know what you mean, Adam."

"She put salt on her food without tasting it first."

"What's wrong with that?"

Adam explained. "You never do that. How do you know it even needs salt? You don't make decisions without first getting all the information. You taste the food first and then you know if it needs salt. What if I stirred the oxygen tanks but didn't stop to see if they needed it? I could blow up the whole spaceship."

"It's not life and death, Adam. It's just salt."

"You don't understand. It might be just salt, but she probably does that with every decision. I can't be with someone like that. She probably makes decisions in every area of her life without first getting the facts."

Courtney made a mental note not to ever salt her food without tasting it.

Adam was right. It didn't have to do with salt. It had to do with something deeper. He wasn't ready to date. Even after all those years.

She turned the volume back up on the press conference. Remembering was getting too hard.

"Toby Collins, New York Times," a tall, thin reporter, with wire-rim glasses said. "What are you going to miss most about earth?"

She caught the subtle hurt on Adam's face. No one else in the room would have noticed it except her. She knew Adam better than he knew himself.

"I'm definitely going to miss the food," Adam said.

The people in the room erupted in laughter.

"Seriously," he continued. "There are too many things to mention. So many people I love and will miss." Adam's tone softened. "I can't explain it really. Six hours from now, I'm going to miss everything. I know it."

Courtney muted the television again. She didn't know which was more painful. Listening or remembering.

Her heart pounded as if someone was ripping it out of her chest. It wasn't like she hadn't known this day was coming. She knew it would be hard, but this was excruciating and almost unbearable.

How could he be leaving me forever? How am I going to live without him?

The night before...

Maybe that was making it harder. Making the loss seem greater. The psychologist in her tried to make sense of her own feelings. *Why did it have to make sense? Of course, she'd feel this way.* Last night was special. She'd never experienced anything like it before. Adam had been vulnerable. She had been willing to give him her heart. They came together at one heartfelt moment. A few minutes in time when two people go inside of each other and become one. Not physically. This was more than that. It was a deeper connection.

Emotional. Spiritual even. Pure love. Not ruined by lustful sex. A love that flowed from the heart.

Words. Looks. Touches. Sharing. Tears...

Adam had told her a secret—something he'd been holding inside. She decided not to hold back either. No longer protect herself from what the next day would bring. She allowed herself to care enough to be devastated.

That's why she was.

They were sitting together on the couch. Courtney took Adam's hand and held it.

"I have a daughter," he blurted out. "Her name is Jamie. She's nineteen."

"You have a daughter?" "How come you never told me about her?"

"I didn't know about her until a couple years ago."

He'd told Courtney about his ex-wife and that she died, but that was all he told her.

"I hadn't spoken to Andrea since the divorce." He started opening up what was obviously a wound. "I came home one day from the university, and there was a note on the kitchen table. It said, 'Sorry. I can't do this. I love you.' That was it. No explanation. No phone calls. I never saw her again. She sent the divorce papers in the mail. I signed them and sent them back."

"How do you know you have a daughter?"

"I saw her at Andrea's funeral."

"You went to the funeral?"

"Yes. I read about her death in the paper. I wouldn't have even known about it except for the obituary. I stood in the back so no one would see me."

"Oh Adam, why would you do that?"

He pulled his hand away. "I didn't know why she left. I didn't know if her family would be mad that I was there. What if Andrea didn't want me there?"

"Why would they be mad? You didn't do anything. She left you."

Adam stood and started pacing.

"Apparently, I did, or she wouldn't have left. Anyway, I saw Jamie at the funeral."

"How do you know she's your daughter?"

Adam opened the sliding glass door that led out to the back deck, still talking as if he expected her to follow him.

Courtney got up from the couch, flipped on the light, and followed him outside.

"I just know. It was obvious. And I did the math. She looks just like my mother." Tears welled up in Adam's eyes. He'd told Courtney his mother and father were killed in a car accident when he was fifteen.

She couldn't imagine what Adam was going through.

"I thought about reaching out to her. I went to her college a few weeks ago. She came out of the dorm, and I was going to tell her but..."

Everything finally made sense to Courtney. The jokes about feelings. The hard, outer shell. The fear of answering the personality tests honestly. Adam's problem wasn't that he had no feelings; he had too many. Too many to bear. He buried them so he wouldn't have to feel them.

The loss of his parents. The loss of his wife. The loss of his daughter. Now, he was going to lose her...

Courtney wasn't being a psychologist on purpose. She was trained to spot these things. And she was being his friend. His lover in the sense that she loved him.

Should I tell him how I feel? Is now the right time? Isn't it obvious? He must already know. Would it make it harder for him? No. Don't tell him. This is about him. His feelings. His losses. Don't make them worse.

He paused a moment and swallowed hard, maybe trying to tamp down his emotions. "I have something for you," he finally said.

"What?"

Adam reached in his back pocket and pulled out an envelope. He handed it to Courtney.

"What is this?" she asked.

"This is everything I owned on earth. I sold it all. It's not going to do me any good now. I don't have any family. I want you to have it."

Courtney opened the envelope and pulled out a cashier's check made out to her for $253,145.78.

She didn't know when her mouth fell open, but she suddenly felt the need to close it. "Adam! You should give this to charity. I can't accept this."

"I did. I gave half of what I sold to several different charities. I wanted you to have the other half."

Courtney felt her knees buckle. She tried to speak but couldn't find any words. *That was the wrong response. You have to accept it. This is his last wish on earth.* She just threw her arms around his neck.

More losses. Everything Adam had on earth was about to be gone. All his possessions. All his friendships. His daughter. *Me.*

How was Adam even coping? She'd been thinking about her pain, but his was even deeper. *He loves me too.* It wasn't a check. He didn't give Courtney his money. He gave her his life. Everything he had. In his own awkward way. Giving himself wasn't an option anymore. For Adam... he was giving her the next best thing. She didn't want the money; she wanted Adam, and he knew it. He wanted her too.

That wasn't going to happen. They both knew what tomorrow would bring, and they were trying to say goodbye in the best way possible. It wasn't quite working. But how could it? These circumstances were too different. No one would know how to say goodbye like this.

She started to pull away, but he held the embrace.

"Maybe you can save it and use it for your daughter someday, if you have one," Adam said, as tears welled up in his eyes.

"I have something for you too," Courtney said, trying to lighten the mood. "You're awfully hard to shop for. What do you get a guy who has his own spacecraft?" She went back inside to the kitchen counter and picked up the wrapped package. Adam followed her back in, and she handed it to him.

Adam opened it.

She watched his reaction to the Bible, looking for anything that might tell her he appreciated it. "Promise me you'll read it. It's the best present I can give you."

"I'll read it. I'll put it beside my bed and will look at it every night before I go to sleep."

It seemed like he meant it.

They'd had many discussions about God and faith. Adam indulged Courtney because he knew how important her faith was, but he never came close to believing. He didn't believe in heaven or in Jesus. That might be her biggest regret. *What if he dies tomorrow having never given his heart to Jesus? I won't even see him in heaven.*

Courtney walked back outside and stood by the porch railing, trying to hide the tears. Maybe distancing herself would make things better. It hadn't worked for Adam and wouldn't work for her either. Her heart felt like someone was dying. In a way, he was. At least, the dream was dead. Whatever the dream was. Maybe if he wasn't going away for good, they could've had a future. Maybe...

As it was, she would never see him again and that was that. This was their last moment together. *He would have to leave soon.*

Adam came up behind her and put his arm around her. "Everything's going to be alright. I'm sorry I have to leave," he said tenderly.

Courtney wiped the tears from her eyes. "Oh right. It's getting late. You're going to have to go. You have a big day tomorrow."

Adam turned Courtney so to face him and said, "That's not what I meant. I'm sorry that I must leave *you* tomorrow. I don't want to..."

He looked into her eyes. Was he going to kiss her? He gazed into her eyes for what seemed like a long time. But not nearly long enough. He pulled her closer.

She fell into his chest.

His heart was pounding.

Maybe it was hers. Maybe it was both of theirs beating in unison. Her tears soaked his shirt.

He stroked her hair.

Lord, why did you bring him into my life to take him away forever?

Then he abruptly pulled away from her, said goodbye, and left.

No kiss to remember him by. No words of "I love you." Though, no words were necessary. They both knew. She had stood on the front porch and watched him drive away. Courtney replayed the whole night repeatedly in her head until she finally fell asleep. The moment was gone. Adam would soon be gone.

She had promised Adam she would go to the launch, but she couldn't do it. It would be too hard. He would never know, and it was just as well. She needed to distance herself from it. Let herself grieve. She didn't resent him for leaving her, but he was, and she had a life to live without him.

* * *

She looked at her watch. The press conference would be wrapping up soon. A mound of tissues was piled on her coffee table.

Courtney stood up from her sofa, stunned. She couldn't believe what happened on the television screen.

Adam had knocked the microphone off the table, pointed his fist angrily at a reporter, and stormed out of the room.

"What in the world just happened?" Courtney asked aloud.

Chapter Four

Today would be Jad Yusaf's last day on earth. He'd known for more than eight months. As a mid-level security guard with NASA for more than ten years, he stood at his post outside the NASA armory staring at the spacecraft they were preparing for the launch in a little over five hours.

A launch he was going to make sure never happened.

He was humbled Allah had called him for such a great moment as this. In his morning prayers, he had prayed, "Allah give us a great victory today against the infidels. Give me courage and lead the way to the battle. I give my life today for your glory."

He ran through his mental checklist one more time after being meticulous in his preparations. Nothing could go wrong now. His last worry had been when the Secret Service searched the armory earlier that morning. They didn't find his FIM-92 Stinger shoulder missile stored in a box in plain view. While the dogs had taken an interest in the box, they were searching in an armory. Of course, there would be munitions and small arms stored there. That was the beauty of the plan. Everything could be easily explained.

Yusaf imagined what the explosion of 318,000 gallons of liquid oxygen would be like when he launched a missile into the fuel tank of Chronos 7. He and everyone within three miles of the explosion would be incinerated almost immediately as if a small atomic bomb went off. More than 200,000 people were expected to be in the blast radius. He didn't care. The spirit of Allah had called him to this moment and would reward him in the life to come with seventy-two virgins. The infidels would be brought to their knees, and he would finally avenge his father's death.

* * *

Courtney trembled as the DVR rewound. She'd never seen Adam angry before. *Why did he storm out of the press conference?* What could possibly have set him off to the extent that he would explode so angrily on worldwide television? She pressed stop.

Adam said, "The speed of light travels at 186,000 miles per second, which equates to 671 million miles per hour. To put that in perspective, the average airplane travels 500-600 miles per hour. I will pass Pluto about eight o'clock tonight."

Courtney had rewound too far.

Administrator Matthews said, "Thank you for being here today. We will take one final question."

She listened carefully. *This must be it.*

"My name is Aaron Fleming from the New York Times. My question is for Commander Lang. Is Jamie Austen your daughter? Her mother's name is Andrea Austen who is your ex-wife. Can you confirm that Jamie is your daughter?"

Courtney gasped.

Adam flung the microphone across the stage and yelled, "This press conference is over!" and then stormed out of the room, shaking his fist at the reporter.

She stared at the television screen trying to process what just happened and all the ramifications. As far as she knew, Sarge was the only other person at NASA who knew about Jamie. NASA wouldn't have selected Adam if they'd known he had a daughter. One of the requirements of the mission was that the astronaut could not have a family. They didn't want any potential entanglements that could jeopardize the mission.

What does this mean?

Courtney thought of all the possible scenarios. Administrator Matthews was going to be furious. *Would he cancel the mission?* What about Adam? How was he feeling at that moment? He'd wanted to tell Jamie, but he wouldn't have wanted her to find out this way. Was Jamie watching the press conference? It wouldn't matter. She would hear about it soon enough.

What a disaster. She had to get to Adam. She quickly dialed his number, but it went straight to voicemail. "Call me. I saw the press conference. Don't do anything rash. I'll be there as soon as I can."

* * *

Adam bolted out of the room. Sarge tried to grab him by the arm as he rushed past him, but Adam pushed him aside. He went down the hall and into the conference room where he had stored his belongings.

Sarge followed him into the room and said, "Man, what are you doing?"

Adam paced the length of the room with his phone in his hand. "Not now. Just turn around, walk out the door, and leave me alone. I need time to think."

"You need to calm down and let's sort this out."

"How did that jerk know about Jamie, and why would he mention her name on live television? You know Jamie's going to hear about it."

"Don't you realize you just made it a lot worse?" Sarge retorted.

"I don't want to hear it," Adam said angrily.

"It was just one reporter who had a suspicion that she might be your daughter. You just confirmed it was true when you flew out of there like a maniac. Now every reporter knows there's a story there, and there's no way they'll let it drop. You should've played it cool and just answered no."

Sarge was right, but Adam hadn't prepared for that question. They had practiced for every imaginable question but that one. He didn't know how to respond at that moment. Who would've known a reporter knew about Jamie, much less have the audacity to say her name in front of two-hundred million people?

What did Jamie have to do with the mission anyway?

The door flew open, and Sarah Reynolds, Administrator Matthews, and Senator Robinson and two of his aides walked in.

"Why didn't you tell us you have a daughter?" John Matthews said in an accusatory tone, his brow furrowed, his lips pulled tightly into a frown.

"I can explain," Adam said.

"How did you pass the lie detector?"

"I didn't know about her when I was first being considered for the program. I just learned about her a few months ago. I swear I didn't know."

"Why didn't you tell us when you found out? You didn't think that was something that we needed to know?" John said.

"She doesn't know about me. I've never met her. I figured it didn't matter. I thought about talking to her, but I never did."

"Well, she knows now. And what was that display out there in front of millions of people. You represent all of us here at NASA. You made a fool of yourself and all of us. I thought you had more sense than that."

"It's not my fault!" Adam said, his voice raising in decibels. "I thought the questions were screened beforehand. Jamie has nothing to do with the mission. I shouldn't have been asked about her."

"How could we know to screen for that question, since you never told us you had a daughter? This is exactly why we don't want any family ties on this mission."

Adam stiffened. "I'm sorry, John. But I didn't know what to do. There was a lot invested in me and this mission. I didn't want to mess it up. I figured no one would ever know, and she would live her life never knowing who I was. I would have told you if I thought it mattered."

"Well, obviously it did matter."

Adam's phone rang. Courtney. *She must have seen the press conference. Everyone saw the press conference.* He sent it to voicemail.

"Everyone just calm down," Sarah said. "This is not helping the situation. What is done is done. What do we do now?"

"We just go ahead with the launch," John answered. "We'll put out a press statement—"

"I'm not going," Adam said. "I have to talk to Jamie."

"You have to go. We have billions of dollars riding on this," Senator Robinson chimed in roughly.

"I'm not going until I talk to her," Adam retorted

"The whole world is watching," John countered. "We have reporters from over a hundred countries here to watch the launch. I'm sorry about whatever is going on with your daughter, but you have a responsibility to all the people who worked hard for you. This mission is bigger than one person."

Adam put his head in his hands. "I can't. I can't live the next thousand years thinking my daughter hates me. She's going to think I abandoned her and her mother. I must tell her the truth. She is going to..."

For the first time since his parents died, Adam cried.

The room remained silent for a good minute. John Matthews didn't get to be the Administrator of NASA without knowing how to take charge of a bad situation. No one saw this coming, but it didn't matter what the crisis was. NASA had seen a lot worse than this, and everyone was trained to set emotions aside and work the problem. A million things could go wrong that day. Both John and

Sarah were capably prepared for any challenge. If anyone could re-solve this, it would be John and Sarah.

Sarah sat down next to Adam and put her hand on his shoulder. "What if we could get Jamie on the phone? We can put her on a video screen, and you can talk to her and tell her whatever you need to say. You can tell her everything. Will that work?"

Adam didn't look up but nodded in agreement. Sarah looked up at John as if asking if they had a solution.

John turned to Senator Robinson, "Is there anything you can do? You can find anybody, right? Can you find Jamie in the next four hours?"

"We actually have more time than that," Sarah said. "It's five hours to launch. Once we launch, Adam still has another hour before he enters the stream. Can you find her in six hours?"

"Surely, the CIA can find her," John answered.

"The CIA can't," Senator Robinson added. "They aren't autho-rized to work on American soil, but the NSA can. They can find anybody in the world in six hours. Adam, tell me what you know about her. What is her full name? Date of birth if you have it? Do you know where she lives? I guess you don't have her cell phone number. That would be too easy. The NSA can find her phone, and they can tell where she is at this very moment within a few hundred yards based on the cell phone ping."

He put his hand to his chin before continuing. "The NSA can get us her number. That is, if it's on. What young girl doesn't have her cell phone on all the time? We might even have time to fly her in, and you can meet with her in person."

Adam perked up. The thought of seeing Jamie in person was something he thought impossible just a few minutes before.

"Her full name is Jamie Ruth Austen. She's nineteen. I don't know her birth date. Here's a picture of her." Adam showed him a picture of her on his phone.

"Great," Senator Robinson said. "Send that to my phone." He gave Adam the number.

"Do you know where she might be right now?" he asked.

"She's a student at George Mason. She lives in Commonwealth Hall. That's probably where she is."

Adam had traveled to George Mason a few months back and sat outside her dorm. He was going to talk to her when she came out in the morning for class. He saw her from a distance but decided not to talk to her. She was laughing and joking with friends, and he figured she was better off not knowing. For whatever reason, her mother didn't want her to know. Even if he disagreed with that, he had to respect her decision. Now he wished he'd talked to her back then.

Senator Robinson turned to his two aides and said to one of them, "Peter, get on this right away. Contact the school and see if they can find her and get her on the phone. Find out the name of her roommate, friends, boyfriend, anybody that might know her and get their number. Don't let them claim they can't give it to you because of privacy. Tell them the President of the United States is making this request, and they had better comply. I'll speak to the President later. One other thing, I imagine a bunch of the press is already calling the school, so this is probably going to be on their radar already. You may have to convince them you are who you say you are and that you are a priority over the others."

Senator Robinson turned to his other aide, "Cathy, call Patrick at NSA and tell him to get the Director on the phone immediately. Tell him it is a national emergency. Tell him I want to know everything there is to know about Jamie Austen. I want her phone number and the location of her phone at this very moment. Give him all the information that Adam just gave you. Tell him time is of the essence."

He continued with urgency in his voice. "Have him look up any credit card charges to see if she's charged anything in the last twenty-four hours. That may also tell us her current location. Have them pull up all her emails and text messages over the last two days. Pull up her social media accounts. See if she's posted anything in the last few hours. Send her a private message and give her my number to call. Tell her it's an emergency. Tell her it's about her father. I want this girl found, and I want her found right now!"

Adam stood and walked over to the Senator. He reached out and shook his hand. "Senator, I can't thank you enough. I will be forever grateful."

"Let's just hope and pray that we find her in time."

Adam thought, "I'll give you some time. If you don't find her, I'm leaving here. I will find her myself."

* * *

10:30 a.m. Four hours and thirty minutes to launch.

Jamie knew all the signs of a concussion. Dizziness, blurred vision, nausea, and severe headache. She had all of those, except nausea, thankfully. She had a severe concussion her senior year in high school when she was the captain of the basketball team, and her head collided with another player of the opposing team. This would be the second in less than a year.

It took her thirty minutes to get out of downtown Miami because her vision was so blurred, she couldn't read the road signs. She stopped at a pharmacy and purchased a bottle of Tylenol and an energy drink. She also rinsed off the dried blood on the back of her head. She had a pretty good-sized bump. Caffeine wasn't good for a concussion, but she needed the energy boost because fatigue was another symptom that was going to hit her as soon as the adrenaline wore off from her confrontation with Fletcher.

She downed five Tylenol and the energy drink, and was already feeling better, except that her head was pounding. She was about three hours from Cape Canaveral. The blurred vision was a huge problem and was making it difficult to drive. She was on I-95 which would take her straight to the right exit, but waves of dizziness and double vision kept coming over her, and she had a hard time staying in her lane. She had barely avoided an accident a few miles back when she started having double vision.

Her phone rang. She looked down and tried to focus on the number. It said unknown caller. She pushed a button she thought was answering the phone, but it disconnected. A few seconds later, it rang again.

Jamie pushed the right button this time. "Hello."

"Is this Jamie Austen?"

"Who is this?" Jamie swerved to get back in her lane.

"This is David Peterson. I'm a reporter with the Herald."

Jamie hung up the phone. *Why is a reporter calling me? Is that the Miami Herald? Does it have something to do with Fletcher? Oh my gosh. Am I in trouble?*

Chapter Five

11:00 a.m. Four hours to launch.

Sarge was pacing like a caged tiger all over the room.

"Sarge, can you sit down?" Adam said, as he raised a glass of water to his lips. "You're making me nervous." They were in a large conference room closer to the launch site and away from the press.

"Sorry. I pace when I get excited. It helps me to think."

"What exactly do you have to think about?" Adam asked sarcastically.

"I'm trying to think of a way to make sure you get on that flight. I thought I was done with you."

"Why don't you go in my place? Oh yeah. That's right. They don't want the whole universe thinking everyone on earth is a complete moron," Adam retorted.

Sarge glared at Adam as he grinned widely.

"You two sound like brothers," Courtney said, as she walked through the open door.

"Courtney," Adam said excitedly.

She walked quickly across the room and threw her arms around him. The others in the room curiously looked their way. He wasn't supposed to have any undisclosed romantic interests either. Adam hugged her back less enthusiastically. He was thrilled she was there but was afraid to show it.

"What are you doing here?" he asked her.

"I saw the press conference and rushed over. The traffic is a nightmare. Did you get my message?"

He realized he forgot to call her back. "Yes. I saw that you called. Sorry, I didn't call you back. It's been a little hectic around here."

The excitement left Courtney's face and was replaced with a puzzled look. Adam detected a hint of hurt as the color drained from her face.

Administrator John Matthews walked in. Adam took a slight step away from Courtney. Sarah and three of her aides were in the room on their phones. They got off them as soon as he walked in.

"Adam, the networks are already reporting that Jamie is your daughter. We figured that was coming. Nothing we can do about that. They asked me for a comment, but I didn't give them one. The press is going crazy with this."

"Welcome to my world," Senator Robinson said.

John turned his focus to Adam. "Sarah and I have decided to delay the launch by twenty-two minutes. That is as long as we can push it out."

With only a couple of times a year when a spacecraft could enter the space stream, Adam knew three-thirty was the latest they could launch and still make the window. After that, they couldn't launch for another few months.

"That gives you an extra twenty-two minutes to find Jamie."

Adam nodded. The Administrator held Adam's gaze as if assessing the mental state of his astronaut.

Adam tried to look composed and determined. He wanted to instill confidence in John that he wasn't going to let him down. The press conference was obviously a huge embarrassment to John, but he would probably never mention it again. The culture of NASA was to not dwell on mistakes.

Courtney squeezed Adam's hand.

Adam quickly moved it away.

She gave him a slight scowl.

Adam pretended not to notice. It pained him to do so. Last night was amazing. He was ruining it. *John would hit the ceiling if he knew I was in love with Courtney. Am I in love with her?*

"Thank you, John," Adam replied.

"How are you holding up?" he asked.

Adam met his eyes. "I'm good. I'm ready to go. The Senator is helping us look for Jamie. Hopefully, I'll be talking to her soon."

Seemingly satisfied, John turned to everyone in the room. "We will be issuing a press statement shortly."

Sarah pointed at the television and everyone turned and looked. Senator Robinson was nearest to the remote, so he took it and turned up the volume. A NASA spokesperson was speaking.

"While we acknowledge that there are a lot of rumors and speculation circulating in the press right now, some of which are true and some that are not true, Adam asks that you respect his privacy and the privacy of Jamie Austen. Jamie, if you are listening to this or if anyone has any information as to Jamie's whereabouts, please call the number on the screen. Thank you."

Senator Robinson muted the television again.

John took a deep breath. "Maybe Jamie is watching. I hope so. Sarah, you need to head on over to Mission Control. Adam, you will stick with the same schedule, just twenty-two minutes later. You will board the spacecraft—a little over two hours from now." John turned and walked out of the room, not waiting for a response.

Sarah and her aides followed him out.

Adam looked over at Courtney. Her demeanor was considerably colder. *I can't let John see that we are anything more than friends. I'm sorry...*

"I should probably go," she said.

Before Adam could reassure her that he desperately wanted her there, Peter, Senator Robinson's aide, burst into the room and said, "Jamie is in Florida!"

"Jamie's here at Cape Canaveral?" Adam said, his pulse rate soaring.

"No. But she's in Florida. I didn't have any luck with the school, but I did get in touch with Jamie's dorm mom." He stopped to catch his breath. "Jamie and several of her friends went to Miami for spring break. She didn't know where they were staying but they weren't supposed to be back until Sunday. So, they may or may not still be there. We think—"

"What about a phone number?" Senator Robinson interrupted. "Did the school give you Jamie's number?"

Peter shook his head no.

"Her contact number has to be in her file," the Senator continued in a matter-of-fact tone. "Schools now have everybody's phone number in one big database so they can text them in case there's a school shooter, a tornado warning, or some other kind of emergency."

"I tried," Peter responded. "They wouldn't give it to me. Just like you said, they claimed it was a privacy issue."

The Senator pursed his lips and rolled his eyes, clearly annoyed with his aide.

Peter looked down at some papers in his hand. "I did find her social media page, and I sent her a private message." His voice got excited again. "The dorm mom did give me the name of her roommate. They went to Florida together. Her name is Rebecca Stevenson. I got her phone number. What do you want to do with it?"

Adam couldn't contain his excitement. That was a very promising development. "Give me the number. I'll call it," Adam said.

Courtney jumped in. "Wait, let me do it. She might be skeptical of a man calling."

I do love you, Adam finally admitted to himself. *What a strange time to feel that.*

Peter gave Courtney the number. She pulled out her phone and dialed it and sat down in the center chair of the conference table.

Adam sat next to her.

Courtney put it on speaker.

Rebecca answered on the third ring.

"Rebecca, my name is Courtney Dixon. I'm trying to get in touch with Jamie Austen. I understand she's with you in Miami on spring break. This is an emergency. Is she with you, and can I talk to her?"

Rebecca paused. "I'm sorry. I'm by the pool. I can't hear you very well; let me step inside so I can hear you better."

"Sounds like there's a party going on behind her," Courtney said.

Adam nodded without expression. Adam was trained not to let his emotions show. That skill had never served him well as far as Courtney was concerned.

She turned her gaze away from Adam in a businesslike manner.

Rebecca came back on and said, "Who is this?"

"This is Courtney Dixon. We've never met, but I'm trying to get in touch with Jamie Austen. This is an emergency. Is Jamie with you?"

"Yes. She is with me. I mean, she's not, like, with me at this moment. She's up in the room."

"Can you go up to the room so I can talk to her?"

"I'm kind of in the middle of something right now. Did you try calling her yourself? We are all, like, going to meet up for dinner later. Can you call back then?"

Courtney's tone got sterner. "What part of 'This is an emergency' do you not understand? This can't wait until dinner. I must talk to her now. I don't have her number, or I would have called her directly. This is very important."

Courtney shifted to the front of her chair and the look on her face was one of pure determination. Adam was glad Courtney was there to handle this conversation.

"Listen to me carefully. Jamie will be extremely upset at you if you don't go to her room right this second and put her on the phone. Can you do that for me?"

Rebecca made a rude sound. "I guess. Give me a minute. I'll call you back."

"No. Don't call me back. Keep me on the line—"

Rebecca hung up.

Courtney hung up her phone, brushed the hair out of her eyes and straightened her blouse without looking at Adam.

Adam's excitement turned to nervousness. "What am I going to say? I've rehearsed this conversation for months. Now that it's here, I don't know what to say."

"Just say what is on your heart," she told him. The warmth returned momentarily.

Cathy, Senator Robinson's other aide bolted into the room and said, "Jamie is at the Beach Street Hotel in Miami. NSA pulled her credit card receipts. She checked into the hotel three days ago. They hacked into the hotel records and confirmed that she is registered in room 425 under her own name." Cathy seemed pleased with herself.

"We already know that," the Senator said. "Her roommate is going up to the room as we speak to get Jamie on the phone."

A disappointed look came over Cathy's face.

Adam wondered if the Senator noticed or even cared. From Adam's perspective, the aides were amazing. The Senator didn't seem satisfied with their efforts.

"Was there anything else?" he said.

"Yes. A 911 call was placed from Jamie's phone about an hour and thirty minutes ago. The call was a woman's voice saying that a man was attacking a young woman in the parking garage of the hotel."

"What?" Adam stood.

"The police arrived and found a man badly beaten with a knife next to him," Cathy continued. "They transported him by ambulance to the local hospital. We're checking with the hospital on his condition right now."

"Did they mention finding a girl at the scene?" Sarge asked.

"No mention of a girl. There was no one else there. Police have no idea who made the call. It definitely came from Jamie's phone, but it will take them a little longer to figure that out."

Before anyone had time to process the new information, Courtney's phone rang. Rebecca's number appeared. She stepped to the center of the room and put it on speakerphone.

"This is Courtney."

"I'm in the room and Jamie is not here," Rebecca said frantically. "I found a note."

"What does the note say?"

"It says, 'I have to go. I'll explain later. Love You. Jay.'"

Courtney looked around the room.

"Rebecca, listen to me very carefully. Do you have any idea where Jamie may have gone?" Courtney said.

"No. I went to the pool, and I wanted Jamie to come, but she said that she, like, had something she wanted to, like, watch on TV. Some kind of a space deal."

They all looked at each other.

"Jamie knows." Adam's heart did a flip flop. He swallowed hard.

"Does Jamie have a car? Could she have left in a car?" Courtney asked.

"Yes. We rented a car at the airport."

"What kind of car is it? Do you know the make and model?"

"I don't remember. I think it was a... I'm not sure."

"Think Rebecca. It's very important. What kind of car was it?"

"It was one of those cars that the top comes down."

"A convertible?"

"No. It was bigger than that. It was like a Jeep."

Adam was frustrated. *How did this girl get into George Mason?*

Senator Robinson turned to Cathy and whispered, "Have the NSA pull the rental car records and find out the make and model. See if the car has a GPS device. We can track it with that."

"Rebecca, I need Jamie's phone number," Courtney said calmly. "Can you look it up and give it to me?"

Rebecca seemed hesitant. "I don't know if I should give it to you."

"Rebecca, this is Senator Joe Robinson. I am the United States Senator from the state of Florida. It's very important that you give us all the information you can about Jamie. I will be personally responsible for this matter."

"Is Jamie in trouble?"

"No. She is not in trouble, but her life may be in danger. It's extremely important that we get in touch with her. What is her cell phone number?" the Senator asked firmly.

Rebecca fumbled with her phone.

"Here it is. Are you ready?"

"Thank you, Rebecca. We are going to try and call Jamie now. Please stay by your phone in case we need to get in contact with you. You did good."

Courtney hung up the phone and said, "Let's call Jamie."

Adam stood up and then sat right back down. Excitement and nervousness, happiness and fear, anticipation and anxiety overwhelmed his senses. *Is it possible to feel so many conflicting emotions at one time?*

Get a hold of yourself. You are finally going to get to talk to your daughter.

* * *

Jamie was making good progress. She was about halfway to Cape Canaveral and traffic was light. She powered up her phone and looked at her maps. According to GPS, traffic around the launch site was at a standstill. The news had said that hundreds of thousands of people were coming to the launch, and it looked like they were getting there early. She'd been thinking about a plan to get around the traffic and into the launch site, but she hadn't come up with anything. Her headache wasn't any better, but the blurred vision had gone away.

Jamie stared at her phone in amazement. Her notifications said that she had 475 missed phone calls, 1263 texts, and 4573 social media notifications.

How is that possible?

"What is going on?" she said aloud. "They must have discovered Fletcher and more reporters are calling me." *Maybe even the police.*

Her phone rang. The caller ID displayed the name Courtney Dixon.

I don't know any Courtney Dixon. She quickly turned the phone back off.

* * *

Back at NASA, Courtney disconnected her phone and said, "It rang, but it went to voicemail, which was full."

Senator Robinson turned to Peter and said, "Have NSA track that phone call and tell me where the phone is?"

"Why is she not answering her phone? I wonder what happened in the parking garage," Adam said nervously.

Senator Robinson turned back to Cathy. "Also, have NSA go into the 911 system and pull up the 911 call that was made from her phone. I want the actual recording. Have them hack into the 911 log and change the incoming number to a burner phone that cannot be traced. I don't know what happened in that parking garage. It's only a matter of time before an investigator looks at those records. I don't want the local police getting in the way of us finding Jamie."

Sarge said, "It seems like Jamie was watching the press conference. If she did, she heard her name."

Adam stiffened. "Maybe she left the hotel and is coming here."

"Let's not get ahead of ourselves," Sarge stated. "She may have been going out to the grocery store for all we know."

Adam shrugged and walked over to the window. "Whatever happened in the garage, Jamie witnessed it but didn't hang around long enough for the police to show up. I think she was in a hurry because she was heading up here."

The Senator held up his hand, silencing the conversation. "Cathy, have them look at the security cameras at the hotel. See if we can see anything in the parking garage."

Cathy turned and walked out of the room just as Peter walked back in.

"Jamie was in Jupiter, Florida, when we made that call to her," Peter said.

Adam slapped his hands together. "She's headed this way. I knew it!"

"Her phone was on at the time," Peter explained further, "but she turned it off right after the call was made."

"Why would she do that?" Adam shook with excitement. No one answered him, so he walked over to where Peter stood.

"Peter," the Senator said with authority. "Get four guys on I-95. Get them Jamie's picture and have them put it on a flyer and go to all the truck stops, rest stops, and gas stations between Jupiter and Port St. Lucie."

He strode over to the conference room table and wrote on a notepad. "She's somewhere between those two towns. I want them to find her." He looked back up from what he was writing. "Have NSA monitor Jamie's phone. If she makes another call, I want to know about it and where she is when she makes it. If she even turns on her phone, let me know right away, and we'll try to call her again. Better yet, get a couple of NSA people in here with computers. I want a direct link to NSA computers from here so we can monitor it in real time."

"I also sent two guys to her hotel room," Peter said. "They should be arriving there any minute. I was going to have them search it and see if they could find anything."

"Good idea," the Senator said as he adjusted his tie. "Have them stay there with Jamie's roommate. Her name is Rebecca. Just in case Jamie calls her. Tell them to detain her and don't let her leave."

Peter started to leave, but the Senator called to him as he headed out the door, "Tell them not to scare her."

Sarge put his hand on Adam's shoulder. Courtney walked over to where Peter and Sarge were standing and whispered, "Must be nice to be a Senator and have that much power."

Adam nodded in agreement. "I'm glad he's on our side."

"God is going to work this together for your good," Courtney told him. "You're finally going to get to talk to Jamie."

Adam didn't know how to respond. He didn't believe in God, but it sure made him feel better when Courtney talked about him. The night before, Courtney said she was praying that Adam would somehow get a chance to talk to Jamie before he left. That seemed impossible at the time. Now, he was wondering if Courtney's prayers were actually working.

How could they work if there is no God?

Chapter Six

11:47 a.m. 3 hours 35 minutes to launch.

Fletcher's dead.

Jamie tightened her grip on the steering wheel. A wave of fear caused the pain in her head to intensify. She could still feel his weight crushing her. His eyes were seared into her memory. They were brown. On fire and filled with hate.

He was going to kill me.

"You didn't have to kill him. You could have run away." Her thoughts looped in her mind like a roller coaster.

"I needed the car and I had to hurry. My dad is leaving." She looked at the clock on the dashboard. Approximately three hours to launch.

"I'm not going to see my dad anyway. There's no way I'll make it in time. They'll never let me into NASA. What was I thinking?"

I was thinking I had to try.

Jamie felt the back of her head. She cringed as she felt the bump and touching it sent pain pulsating through her whole body.

"You are going to jail."

She shook her head. "No. He had a knife. He was stalking me. He deserved it." Every detail came flooding back. His smell, the sweat on his forehead, his shirt drenched, his clammy hands... horrendous breath. Each exhale blew the stench in her face as he pummeled her with punches. Jamie brushed off her shirt and shuddered as if remnants of the monster were still on her.

He was so strong. He said something. What was it?

"I'm going to kill you!"

The fear assaulted her all over again. "That was it. He said he was going to kill me as he was hitting me. He would have raped me and then killed me."

I did the right thing. Kill or be killed. I would rather die than let him touch me. I'll tell that to the jury.

Jamie made a disgusted face. *Ewww.* "The thought of him kissing me... Touching me."

"Anyone else would do the same thing. Surely they'll believe me."

But I ran... Makes me look guilty.

Jamie tensed. A police car sat along the side of the road a half a mile ahead. She slowed to below the speed limit. *They probably know my car by now.*

"Just keep your cool. You are a long way from Miami. They aren't looking for you all the way up here."

Jamie passed the policeman and resisted the urge to look his way. She kept glancing in the rearview mirror, praying that he would stay there. He did at first.

He's moving.

He settled in behind her. It was all she could do to not scream.

"He's running my license plates. Any second now, he'll know it's me."

Should I try to outrun him?

Don't be stupid. That'll only make things worse.

Jamie began to cry. "I'm never going to talk to my dad."

I'm sorry. Mom.

He followed her for more than a mile. *Why isn't he pulling me over?*

The policeman pulled into the next lane and passed Jamie. She let out a huge breath. Her chest hurt from holding it in.

"You're just being paranoid. You don't even know that Fletcher is dead."

Her phone had been charging on the center console. She picked it up, turned it on, but didn't look at the number of notifications. She didn't want to know.

"I'll call Rebecca. If the police are looking for me, they would have contacted her by now." *Please be by the pool sunning yourself.*

Jamie searched her favorites in the phone contacts. Her hands shook as she placed the call.

"Becca, it's me, Jamie."

Rebecca whispered, "Jay, are you okay. I have been worried sick about you."

Why is she whispering? "I'm okay. I'm on my way—"

"Are you in some kind of trouble?"

Jamie grimaced.

"There are two men in our hotel room asking all kinds of questions. They wanted your cell phone number. I gave it to them. I hope you're not mad at me."

Jamie slammed her hand against the steering wheel.

What do I do? What do I say?

A man came on the phone and said, "Jamie, we need to talk to you."

She hung up.

How did they find me so fast? There must have been cameras in the garage.

"Fletcher is definitely dead. I shouldn't have hung up. It was self-defense. They could see that on the cameras. Hanging up makes me look guilty of something. I need to turn myself in."

Jamie's phone rang. It was Becca. She quickly turned the phone off.

"If I turn myself in, I won't be able to talk to my dad. I have to see him. I have to talk to him. I promised." It was the only justification she could think of that they might believe. *It's the truth.*

Jamie rolled down the window and started to throw her phone out. She hesitated. "If the phone is off, they can't track it. I need to keep it. I might need it later."

She rolled the window back up.

"Pull yourself together." She pulled down the sun visor and flipped open the mirror. It showed the fear in her eyes. They were bloodshot from crying.

Stop it. Crying isn't going to help anything.

"I'm less than an hour from Kennedy. I just have to focus and get to my dad."

Eat something. I'm going to need my strength.

She took the protein bar from her bag and scarfed it down. The bottled water was warm but soothed her parched and dry throat. She drank both. A couple of deep breaths calmed her heartbeat. She quickly unwrapped a piece of gum and stuck it in her mouth. It tasted good.

What's that sound?

An alarm was beeping in her car. A warning light was flashing. She was out of gas.

"Great! That's just what I need. Run out of gas in the middle of nowhere."

* * *

12:01 *3 hours and 21 minutes to launch.*

Senator Robinson introduced the two men as investigators for the NSA. The NASA holding room had been turned into an electronic war room. Sophisticated computers and equipment were connected by dozens of wires. A satellite phone with a secure line allowed them to speak directly to NSA headquarters. Every effort was being made to find Jamie. Each passing minute created more urgency.

One of the men began speaking. The Senator had mentioned their names, but Adam couldn't remember what they were. He asked Sarge and learned that one was Brandon and the other was Don.

"Here is what we know," Brandon said. Of the two, Brandon was clearly the one in charge.

Courtney, Adam, and Sarge sat around the conference table. After introducing the men, Senator Robinson poured himself a cup of coffee and sat down in a lounge chair in the corner of the room. Adam was too nervous to eat or drink anything.

"Jamie was at the Beach Street hotel in Miami watching the press conference according to Rebecca, her roommate," Brandon continued. "We assume she heard her name mentioned because she left her room less than five minutes after the press conference was over. The security camera from the fourth floor in the hotel confirmed that fact. We see Jamie walking through the lobby two minutes later. Don, pull up the footage."

Everyone turned and looked at the television screen. An image of a young woman walking through the hotel lobby appeared.

"That's her!" Adam said excitedly. "That's Jamie."

"She's beautiful," Courtney said.

Adam nodded in agreement. Jamie was wearing white shorts, a yellow t-shirt, and sneakers. Her shoulder length, blonde hair flowed with her perfectly proportioned, tall, athletic build. She walked confidently and went straight into the gift shop.

"She emerged from the gift shop with a bag in her hand and walked to the parking garage elevator. I want you to focus your attention on the man to the left, behind the trees." Brandon pointed at the screen.

Adam stood up and walked over to the television for a closer look. "Who is he?"

"He is the man in the hospital. The one who was assaulted. His name is Matt Fletcher. He's an employee of the hotel."

"Can you back it up? He is looking right at Jamie."

"Right. It's clear from the footage that he's fixated on her. He starts to follow her into the elevator. But notice that he turns around abruptly and heads for the stairs. He's clearly acting suspiciously."

"Do those stairs lead to the parking garage?" Sarge asked.

"They do. We think he followed Jamie into the garage. You can see he's in a hurry as well. Don, back up the tape again. Look at Jamie's reaction when she sees him. Notice how she rushes into the elevator, clearly trying to avoid him." The screen showed Fletcher getting to the elevator just as it was closing and then rushing over to the door to the stairs.

The anxiety caused the muscles in Adam's shoulders and neck to tighten. His heart did somersaults in his chest. What was he seeing? He'd been in the most nerve-wracking situations imaginable. But they were nothing compared to this.

"What happened in the garage?" Sarge asked.

Brandon shrugged his shoulders and shook his head. "This is where things get sketchy. There are no cameras in the garage. We assume Jamie went to the garage to get her car, and Fletcher followed her down there. At that point, there was a confrontation of some sort. Fletcher was badly beaten by someone. A knife was found close to his body, but he didn't have any stab wounds. It may have been his knife or the attacker's. We just don't know. He is in pretty bad shape and is in surgery as we speak. He is expected to live, but someone did a number on him. He won't be able to tell us anything for a while."

"Do you think he attacked Jamie? On the 911 call, Jamie said she saw him attacking another woman. She didn't say he was attacking her."

"It sure looks like he was following Jamie, but we aren't sure who he was attacking or who took him down. Apparently, Jamie wasn't the one who was attacked. According to the 911 call, she just saw the attack."

"Where is the woman who was attacked?" Sarge asked the obvious unanswered question.

"I couldn't tell you. I told you things are sketchy. No one has found the woman. Jamie didn't leave the lobby with anyone else. We don't see anyone coming or going into the garage from the lobby around that time. Jamie could have been meeting someone in the garage. A man perhaps. He might have been the one who beat up Fletcher."

"That Fletcher guy looks huge," Courtney said.

"He weighs well over three hundred pounds. It would take a pretty strong person to beat him up that badly. Especially if the knife was his, and he intended to use it."

"There had to be another man in the garage," Sarge said.

Adam responded, "Jamie didn't mention a second man. She just said that a man was assaulting a woman. Maybe Fletcher came to Jamie's aide and somebody assaulted him. But why say it was another woman if it was her?"

"My best theory," Brandon said, "is that Fletcher tried to assault another woman, probably not Jamie, and someone intervened. That someone stopped the attack, and the man and woman left the garage. Based on the size of Fletcher and the extent of his injuries, it had to be another man. Jamie saw the attack and phoned it in."

"Why didn't she want to leave her name?" Adam asked.

"I have no idea. It's all speculation. We just don't know what happened."

Adam was a man who didn't like speculation. He wanted the facts. The facts didn't make sense.

"Adam, would you recognize Jamie's voice?" Brandon said.

"I would. I heard her speak at her mom's funeral."

"Listen to this 911 call and tell me if it's Jamie's voice." Brandon motioned to Don. Shortly thereafter, a woman's voice filled the room.

"This is 911. What is your emergency?"

"A man is assaulting a woman on the second floor of the parking garage at the Beach Street hotel. There are injuries, so send an ambulance. When the EMTs arrive, tell them that the man has an orbital fracture, and there may be hemorrhaging of the brain. Please hurry!"

"What is your name?"

The tape ended abruptly with no answer to that question.

Adam had nodded immediately but waited until the end of the recording to speak. "That is definitely Jamie. I recognize her voice." His voice cracked as he spoke.

"Good. At least we know that she was alive at that point," Brandon said.

Adam raised his voice in panic. "What do you mean she is alive? Do you have any reason to believe that she's dead?"

"No. That's not what I meant. All I'm saying is that Jamie was apparently not the woman who was being assaulted in the parking garage. She saw what happened and called 911, but she was already in her car, so she wasn't the one attacked."

Don interrupted Brandon with urgency. "Jamie just placed a call to Rebecca a few minutes ago. We have an agent on the scene. He tried to talk to Jamie, but she hung up as soon as he got on the phone."

"Why would she do that?" Sarge asked.

Senator Robinson stood and walked over to look at the computer. "Did Rebecca confirm it was Jamie?"

Don nodded.

"That's good news. At least we know she is alive. Where was she when the call was made?"

Don typed something into the computer. "The call was made just south of Port St. Lucie. Right here. He pointed to something on the screen."

"That's about an hour south of here. Do we have any men near there?"

"Let me check." Don picked up his phone and dialed a number. After a brief conversation, he hung up the phone and said, "Yes. We have two men right around that area. They've been canvassing gas stations. But they haven't seen her, and no one else has either."

The Senator said, "Tell them to keep looking. She's in the vicinity. Give them the mile marker where the call was made. Hopefully, she has to stop for gas or use the restroom."

"Did you ever find out the car rental information?" Sarge asked.

"No," Brandon said. "We're having trouble getting into the rental car company's computers. We can go into them, but we can't locate her reservation. Rebecca said it was a red Jeep, but we don't know the license plate number."

"Is her phone still on?" the Senator asked. "We could try calling her again."

"She turned it off right after the call."

"Tell them to be on the lookout for a red Jeep. There couldn't be too many of them on the road." Senator Robinson went back and sat down in his chair.

Adam hovered over the conference table. "Is it possible that Jamie was the person who was assaulted?" Adam wondered aloud. "Why is she afraid to answer her phone or talk to anyone? Something happened in that garage that made her afraid. What is it?"

"That's what we don't know," Brandon said.

"What if she was kidnapped? What if Fletcher had a partner in the garage, and he turned on him, beat him up, and grabbed Jamie?" Sarge said.

Adam glared at Sarge. "Why would she call 911 if she'd been kidnapped?" he interjected. "They would've just gotten out of there as quickly as possible."

"And why would she call Rebecca?" Courtney asked. "A kidnapper wouldn't let her call her roommate."

"Yeah. That doesn't make sense," Sarge said. "I agree. Sorry Adam."

"Also, why would she be on I-95," Brandon surmised. "It's too big a coincidence. She's clearly heading this way. Why she doesn't want to talk to anyone is a mystery."

"What if Jamie was the one who beat up Fletcher?" Adam said, trying to think of all possible scenarios. "Maybe, he attacked her; she beat the heck out of him and didn't want to wait for the police because she was in a hurry to get here. She called 911 because she knew he was badly hurt."

"That's right," Sarge said excitedly. "How would Jamie know Fletcher had an orbital fracture?"

Adam beamed with pride. "She knew because she was the one who caused it."

Chapter Seven

Jamie drove five miles before she came to an exit with a gas station. She gave a huge sigh of relief, but a shot of adrenaline coursed through her veins as she looked at the clock and remembered that time was still her worst enemy. A quick glance around the parking lot, reassured her that no police cars were there. She did notice a four-door sedan with an NSA license plate that looked somewhat like an unmarked police car, but it didn't trigger concern. The NSA was a government agency. They didn't have any reason to be looking for her.

As soon as she stepped out of the car, the dizziness returned like a tidal wave. She grabbed the side of the door to prevent a fall. It took a moment to regain her balance enough to walk. Jamie waited for the dizziness to pass before stumbling over to the fuel dispenser. Because of the blurred vision, she needed several tries to get the credit card in line to go into the slot.

Jamie hesitated. Credit card purchases can be tracked.

The sign on the pump said that fuel had to be prepaid. Cash was acceptable but had to be taken inside. Once inside, the large "restrooms" sign reminded her that her bladder had been screaming at her for more than a half hour. The short break in the restroom from the troubles did her good. She splashed cold water on her face, which invigorated her. Paper towels folded together, wetted with icy cold water, and placed on the sizable bump on the back of her head, brought immediate, if only temporary, relief.

"What a crazy day you have had," she said to herself in the bathroom mirror. "Let's hope it's worth it, and I get to see my dad." For the first time in hours, her nerves were somewhat calm.

The restrooms were in a narrow hallway off the main counter. As she exited the bathroom, she stopped in her tracks. An unsettling feeling welled up inside. A sixth sense. Something was wrong with the picture, and the concussion was taking her longer to process the visuals in the environment as quickly as normal.

Two men in black suits stood at the counter holding a piece of paper, showing it to the attendant.

Jamie's heart pounded at a rapid pace. She strained to hear what they were saying.

"Have you seen this girl?" one of the men said, pointing at the picture on the flyer.

The attendant had a heavy accent, but his words were clear. "No. I haven't seen her. Who is she?"

"Look again. Her name is Jamie Austen. Have you seen this girl?" he said with more emphasis.

Jamie held her hand over her mouth to keep from screaming. Her head started pounding again as the blood pumped faster through her brain from the elevated heart rate. She shook her head violently from side to side as her vision blurred again. Her hands shook...

Panic. Confusion. Fear...

What do I do...? Who are they? Wait for them to leave. They haven't seen me.

"I'm going to go take a leak," one of them said. The men's restroom was right next to where she stood.

I have to get out of here.

A quick scan of the surroundings showed no exit other than the way she had come in. He was approaching quickly. The hallway was only a few steps from the counter. Too late to go back into the women's room. She turned her back and hid her face.

He opened the door to the men's room but paused. "Jamie. Is that you?" he asked.

Her reaction was spontaneous and swift. Instinctive. Without thought of the consequences. A rapid spin. A roundhouse kick connected in his midsection before he could react. The air rushed from his body as he staggered backward and let out a loud grunt.

Jamie rushed out of the hallway and pushed aside the other man in the suit as he ran toward her. She was out the door before anyone knew what was happening.

She fumbled for the keys as one of the men came running out of the station.

"Jamie, wait!" he shouted.

She opened the door, jumped in, and somehow got it locked just as the man reached the passenger door and tried to open it. He banged on the window.

"Please," he pleaded. "We are with..."

Whatever he was yelling, she wasn't paying attention.

She sped away, her thoughts racing faster than the Jeep. She was afraid to look back.

"Who were those men? They weren't policemen. They must be the FBI. Why would the FBI be looking for me?"

I just assaulted an FBI agent.

"I killed Fletcher. Now I've assaulted an FBI agent. And I'm resisting arrest."

What other charges can we add to the list?

For a moment, the fear turned into resolve. "They're *not* going to catch me. I won't let them take me alive."

"Shut up, Jamie. Don't be stupid. You're in a lot of trouble. This isn't a movie. You aren't a heroine."

"I've come this far. I can't give up now. They may catch me, but I'm going to do everything I can to see my dad."

She raced onto the freeway, this time ignoring the speed limit. She had less than an hour's drive to Kennedy Space Center, and she still had three hours to get there. More adrenaline as a new revelation hit her. There weren't three hours left. Dad would be going onto the spacecraft at any time, and she wouldn't be able to see him. It may already be too late. He may already be on there.

Doesn't matter. I have come this far. I have to keep going.

Jamie was quickly running out of options. The odds of her making it in time to see her father were dwindling by the minute. It was complicated by an army of law enforcement looking for her and the red Jeep. Ditching the car was an option, but that would waste even more time.

The car began to sputter. "I didn't get gas!" She pounded the steering wheel.

Jamie barely managed to steer it to the side of the road and out of the traffic as it shut off.

She started to cry but caught herself.

No. I'm not going to cry. Think. What would Dad do?

Thoughts now poured into her head as fast as she could process them. The men would no doubt be on the road after her by now. They could easily call for backup, and the road ahead would have roadblocks looking for her and the Jeep. She needed to get out of the car and as far away from it as possible.

Jamie swallowed hard. This was risky. The more she ran the worse things had become. She could wait in the car and it would be over soon. They would find her in no time.

"Turn yourself in. That's the best thing you can do. You're making things worse." She shook her head. *No. I promised my mom and I'm going to keep my promise. I have to try and see my dad.* The man at the station wasn't hurt that badly. *I took something off the kick on purpose.*

I didn't want to hurt him, I just wanted to slow him down. It just knocked the air out of him.

"Good luck telling that to the authorities."

"But they never said they were the authorities. They weren't wearing uniforms. They have to identify themselves, don't they? I thought he was attacking me like Fletcher did. The other man chased me to the car and tried to open my door. He didn't show a badge. Doesn't he have to show a badge?"

"I was scared for my life."

She closed her eyes. The more intense the thoughts, the greater the intensity of the headache. Rubbing her temples helped if only for a moment. *I have to decide.*

"Wait for the men. They might take you to your dad."

No. She couldn't take that chance. Jamie made her decision. She gathered up what she needed and put everything in the plastic gift-shop bag. To the right were trees, perfect for hiding, but there wasn't time for that. She got out, locked the Jeep, and started walking as fast as she could on the shoulder.

Get as far away from the car as fast as you can.

She started running. Each stride on the pavement sent shock-waves of pain echoing through her concussed head. Sprinting was her forte on the high school track team. Within three minutes, she was half a mile away.

She stopped running and turned to look. The Jeep was barely visible in the distance but was close enough for her to see a cream-colored, four-door sedan pull off the highway and stop behind the Jeep. Two men in suits, who looked like the same ones at the gas station, got out of the car, split up, and walked to each side of the car, peering in the windows.

A large semi-truck passed by and pulled off onto the shoulder ahead of her. Jamie glanced back. One of the men was looking in her direction. He was barely visible, and she figured he could barely see her as well. She walked to the truck and stood a good distance from the door. The window was down.

"Do you need a ride?" a man asked in a friendly voice.

Jamie glanced back and saw one of the men pointing in her direction.

"Sure." She stepped up on the cab, opened the door, and hopped inside."

I hope I haven't made a huge mistake getting in this truck with a total stranger.

* * *

12:15 p.m. 3 hours 7 minutes to launch

The conference room at NASA had quieted down considerably. They hadn't heard anything about Jamie for a while. Courtney was on the phone sitting in the corner of the room. Adam stood and headed for the door.

"Where are you going?" Sarge asked.

"I'm going to the lady's room to powder my nose."

"I have to go with you," Sarge said. "Sarah told me not to let you out of my sight."

"Seriously. You're going to go to the john with me. What are we... girls? I like you but not that much."

"I have my orders not to let you out of my sight."

"I'm going to be spending some time in one of the stalls. If you want to keep me in your sights, be my guest."

Sarge's eyes widened. "I think I'll pass. I'm not getting combat pay for this."

"Good choice. Sit down and take a load off. I'm not going anywhere. I might not be right back, if you know what I mean, but I'll come back as soon as I'm finished."

Adam had spent the last thirty minutes considering his options. Jamie obviously knew about him and was trying to get to Cape

Canaveral. For whatever reason, she was avoiding her phone. It had to have something to do with what happened in the parking garage. If she thought she was in trouble for leaving the scene, it would probably feel to her like she was on the run. The confrontation with Fletcher had to be self-defense. Why would she attack him? He was the one following her.

He also wasn't convinced that Jamie would make it in time. He had to get out of this mission. Running away wasn't an option. Adam was too practical for that. Too many people worked too hard for him to selfishly let them down in that way. Something had to be done to delay the launch. Something that no one would expect he was behind. He went into the men's room and locked the door behind him, taking out his phone in the process. He pressed a number in his favorites he'd called a thousand times.

A man answered on the first ring. "Brayton."

"Carl. It's Adam."

Carl Brayton was the Operation's Manager for this mission. He'd been with NASA for thirty-plus years and knew more about the internal workings of the spacecraft than any man alive. If there was a problem, he was the one who knew how to fix it. Adam had spent more than 2,000 hours in the simulator, and Carl had been there for each one.

"How are you doing, brother? You should be getting on the spacecraft soon. How are things working out with your situation?" Carl asked.

"It's not over yet. That's why I'm calling. I need a favor, and you're not going to like it."

He laughed. "I never like it when someone starts a sentence with 'I need a favor.' What do you need?"

"Is it possible for you to cause a glitch in the software right before launch that would postpone it, but no one would know it was anything more than a malfunction?" Adam asked hesitantly.

"I don't like where this conversation is going."

"I told you that you wouldn't like it."

The phone went silent. Adam was the first to break the silence "About ten minutes to launch, if I haven't talked to my daughter, I need for you to create a false warning light. It has to be some kind of problem that can't be fixed in ten minutes. Something serious enough that Sarah will have to shut down the mission."

Carl's tone changed. So did his volume. He lowered his voice, clearly not wanting anyone else to hear his side of the conversation. "Are you crazy? I can't do that. I would lose my job, my pension. I might even be arrested."

"You won't lose your job. No one will know it was you. Can't you cover your tracks, so it doesn't look like sabotage? Even if it did, no one would ever suspect you."

"Adam. A lot is riding on this mission. You've spent months preparing. We've worked too hard to throw it all away now."

"You have a daughter, man. Imagine what it would be like if you had never talked to her before, and you were never going to be able to talk to her again. I have to explain to her what happened."

"I feel for you, but that's too much to ask."

"How would you feel if you were going away forever and didn't have a chance to say goodbye?"

Carl didn't respond.

"Come on, Carl," Adam implored. "It probably won't even be necessary. We're looking for Jamie right now, and she'll probably make it in time. Make the glitch so it will activate only if she doesn't."

"Lang, I would do anything for you. You know that. I just can't do what you're asking."

"Promise me you'll at least think about it," Adam begged.

"You can still talk to her after the launch. You have an hour."

"I know. But what if she doesn't make it in that hour? I have to stop the launch. Once I'm in space, it will be too late. I'll enter the space stream and be gone forever."

The phone was silent again.

"What's the big deal?" Adam said. "So, we'll launch in six months. We aren't cancelling the mission, just delaying it. Delays happen all the time."

"How will I know if you've talked to her?" he said with a tone of resignation.

Adam sensed that he might do it. He knew it was a long shot when he first devised the plan, and that question told Adam that Carl was considering it.

"At exactly ten minutes to launch," Adam answered, hope growing inside him, "I'll tell Sarah a corny astronaut joke. You know, that banter we have going back and forth. That will be your cue that I haven't talked to Jamie. If I don't tell the joke, we're good for launch. Okay. Will you do that for me?"

"I'm going to regret this, but yeah, I'll do it. Let me rephrase that. I will think about it."

"Thanks man. I owe you one."

Carl laughed nervously, "How am I ever going to collect it from you?"

If this works, I will still be here, and you can collect all you want.

* * *

Yusaf had been disappointed when he heard on the radio the launch had been delayed by twenty-two minutes. That was nothing unusual. He'd witnessed dozens of launches, and delays were frequent if not expected. A flock of seagulls landed on the rocket and launch pad, and he smiled. "You don't want to be around here in three hours, little birds."

He had no doubts about what he was doing. His Sheikh, Abu Mohammad Bashara, preached that forgiveness was a virtue. However, his trainer in Somalia had said that he was a warrior and that forgiveness was a weakness.

His hatred for Americans began thirty-seven years before when his father was killed in a drone strike in Galkayo, Somalia. The Americans had called his father, "collateral damage." A drone sent a missile that struck the building housing his father's carpentry business. The target was a group of al-Shabaab rebels who ran into the building to hide from the US attack. His father was killed along with eighteen rebels.

His mother brought him to America as a boy, and they had received asylum. They both became US citizens several years later. He lived most of his life in America. While he believed that most Americans were good people, it was their country's war against Muslims that had stoked his ire. America had been killing Muslims for more than sixty-plus years. Now was the time for Muslims to strike back. September 11, 2001 had been the last truly successful Muslim attack. That would pale in comparison to this one.

"I will kill more Americans today than they have killed of my people in sixty years. And there is nothing anyone can do about it now."

Chapter Eight

1:00 p.m. - 2 hours 22 minutes to launch

NASA arranged for a buffet lunch to be brought in for every-one. Senator Robinson left to meet the Vice President and First Lady who had arrived for a reception at one o'clock. Adam was to meet them at one-thirty shortly before entering the spacecraft.

Courtney and Sarge helped themselves to the buffet, although Courtney barely took anything. What she did take was left largely uneaten on her plate.

Adam had been given the opportunity to have anything he wanted brought in by special order. He jokingly called it his "Last Supper."

Courtney said that wasn't funny.

Adam ordered two peanut butter and jelly sandwiches, macaroni and cheese, and a piece of chocolate pie, with chocolate milk to drink.

"What are you—twelve?" Sarge said jokingly.

"Shut up," Adam replied. "These are my favorite foods."

"Not me, man. If I was having my last meal, I'd have a huge porterhouse steak. I'd want French fries... no wait... a large baked potato with everything on it, no... garlic mashed potatoes with cheese on them. Give me all three for my last meal. And a big pile of broccoli, and a lobster tail with dipping sauce. I would also want apple pie with ice cream on it."

"They'd have to cart you out to the spacecraft," Adam said, looking at Courtney for any reaction. She didn't even look up as she pushed her food around her plate without taking a bite.

"What about you, Courtney? What would you want for your last meal?" Sarge asked.

"Can we change the subject?" Courtney said, blinking back tears.

Everyone sat in silence for several minutes.

"I wonder if they've heard anything more," Adam said, finally breaking the silence.

The two NSA men were meeting in a separate room on a conference call. An hour ago, Jamie's Jeep was found abandoned along I-95 just south of Port St. Lucie, but she was nowhere to be found. They'd heard nothing since. How had she vanished into thin air?

"I guess not, or we would have heard something," Sarge said.

Where are you Jamie?

Sarge excused himself and left Adam and Courtney alone in the conference room.

"You're being very quiet," Adam said as he leaned back in his chair.

"Yeah, well, I'm sorry. I don't know how I'm supposed to act," she said curtly.

He didn't say anything for a moment. What could he say? "I'm glad you're here," he blurted out.

"Are you? You don't act like it," she said with as much hurt in her voice as anger.

"What do you mean? Of course, I'm glad you came. What's wrong?"

She hesitated before finally saying, "Last night meant something to me."

"It meant something to me too."

"What did it mean to you?" Her anger intensified. "Since we met, you've shut me out of that part of your life. Last night, you let me in. Today, you shut me out again. How do you turn it on and off so easily?"

"I'm sorry. I don't know how to relate to you with people from NASA around. John was furious about Jamie. He would've hit the ceiling if I had told him about us."

"There is no us... There never has been. There never will be—"

"What do you want from me? You've always known we didn't have a future. In twenty minutes, I'm saying goodbye to you forever."

Didn't she understand he couldn't allow himself to get close to anyone?

"You don't think I know that? You don't think... I cried myself to sleep last night, knowing that I would never see you again. Then the press conference happened, and I rushed over here to be with you. I wanted to help you. You act like this. It's hard for me."

"What do you want me to say?" he implored.

"Nothing. Just say nothing. That's what you always do."

"What are you talking about?"

"You never say how you feel. You shut down rather than saying what you feel. You're going away forever. I get that. It's hard for you too. I know it is. But why can't you just say that. Don't you have any feelings for me? You don't have anything you want to say to me before you're gone forever?"

"I've never been good at sharing my feelings."

"No! Stop it. I'm not letting you get off that easily. That's just an excuse. It's hard for all of us. It's hard for me right now to tell you how I feel. But I have to do it. If you don't say what you feel, then everybody thinks you don't feel anything. If you don't feel anything for me, fine. Don't say anything. But I know you have feelings for me. I just don't know how to handle the silence. The distance is excruciating. I'm just being honest with you. I've never felt this way before. I'm sorry. I thought you felt the same way."

She buried her face in her hands and cried.

Adam stood, walked around the conference table, and sat next to her. The gesture was awkward. She didn't turn and face him. Her hands were covering her eyes, so he couldn't hold them. His hand on her shoulder seemed inappropriate for the moment, too impersonal, too superficial, something a friend would do. He was more than a friend. He only had to figure out how to let her know it.

"Never mind. Forget I said anything. I'm talking too much. I'm sorry." Her words were muffled.

"You need to quit apologizing." He reached out and put his arm around her. She pulled away, stood, and walked over to the window.

"Why are you doing this? I thought last night was special too. I don't want our last moments together to be like this," Adam said.

"It doesn't matter. You're right. You are leaving soon. I'm sorry. I know you have a lot on your mind. You don't need this. You don't have any feelings. I just have to accept it."

"You don't think I have feelings?" Adam said angrily. "You don't think I'm going to miss you? Do you think this is easy for me?"

"How would I know?" her voice raised with purpose. "You never say how you feel. You just act like everything is okay. Well it's not okay. I'm going to miss you. I think you'll miss me too. How would anybody know? You won't say. I just wish you would say how you really feel about me. Like you did last night when you talked about how you felt about Jamie. You said you were going to miss her. You obviously love her. You never said you were going to miss me. You never said you love... me."

Walls. His. Adam wanted to break them down; he just didn't know how.

The large windowpane framed his spacecraft perfectly as it sat majestically like an eagle on the launch pad. This was the best vantage point from all of NASA.

Courtney stood staring at it.

Adam stepped closer to the window but remained a few feet from her. Giving her a little space.

Finally, the words came.

"Do you know why I signed up for the mission two years ago?"

"No."

"I signed up because I had nothing on earth to live for," his voice cracked. "Nothing. I hated my life. My wife had left me. All I had was being an astronaut. And I was good at it. But I don't have to tell you that being an astronaut is a lonely existence."

Adam took a moment to let that sink in.

"Do you know what most astronauts talk about when they're in space?" Adam said that more accusingly than he'd meant to.

"No," she said.

Adam softened his tone. "When they aren't talking about the mission, they're talking about all the things they miss on earth. One guy told me that the worst two days of the mission for him were the last two. You want to know why? Because he couldn't stand the wait. He wanted to get home so badly, the last two days were miserable."

"I could see that."

"You know what the worst day was for me?"

"What?"

"The last day."

"Why? That was the day you came home."

"Exactly. Unlike all the other guys, I had nothing to come home to. I didn't want to come back to earth. I dreaded the thought. There was nothing here for me. Most guys couldn't wait to get home to their families and friends. We would land, and all their families were waiting for them in the welcoming room. Do you know who met me when we landed? Nobody. Everybody else had wives, girl-friends, kids, friends, mothers. Me, I had nobody."

"I never knew."

"It's lonely in space, even being with the other astronauts. When we were in space, guys would talk about how lonely it was being away from their families. When I was up there it wasn't any differ-ent for me than when I was on earth. It felt just as lonely down here as it did up there. I figured that if I was going to be lonely, I might as well be trying to accomplish something."

Courtney started to speak, but Adam stopped her.

"Let me finish," he said gently. "The mission gave me something to live for. Something to accomplish. I could make something of my life. I didn't have any kids. My parents were dead. My grandparents died when I was young. I was an only child, so I have no brothers or sisters. There was nothing on earth keeping me here. I wasn't dating anyone. I have only been on one date since my divorce, and you know how that turned out."

Adam choked back the tears. "I thought maybe out there I could find my purpose in life. Now, I don't know."

Courtney stepped closer. They still weren't touching, but the dis-tance between them was receding, emotionally and physically.

Courtney folded her arms in front of her.

Adam reached over and unfolded them. Her fists were clenched. He unclenched them. Tears were streaming down his face. Hers as well. They had nothing to wipe them away, so they ignored them.

"Now I would give anything to not have to go..."

"I think I understand," Courtney said sweetly.

His floodgates were now open. "Before I had nothing," he contin-ued. "Now I have you. Maybe I have Jamie. I don't know."

He looked out at the spacecraft.

"Two hours from now, that ship is sailing. I have to be on it." They could see the crowd of people gathering in the distance and over by Mission Control. Reporters had already begun jockeying for the best position in the press area. The grandstands were nearly full.

"All those people are counting on me to get on that spacecraft and give them a show. They don't care if I'm going to miss you. They don't care that I have to spend a thousand years alone, never seeing you again. They don't know or care how hard it's going to be."

"I know. I care."

"Do you want to know why this is so hard?"

"Why?"

This time there was no hesitation. "Because I love you, Courtney. I know that now. I will miss you so much. It's too painful to even talk about. I can't even express in words how much I'm going to miss you. I haven't allowed myself to think about it because the pain would be so unbearable. And there is nothing I can do about it."

In one moment, a second even, his lips were on hers. He could feel her warmth, her passion, her breath as she relaxed her lips and kissed him back, both giving themselves completely to the moment. Their eyes were open, piercing each other, penetrating deep into each other's souls.

Passion. Intensity. Electricity. It was pure. Love. As quickly as it happened, it was over.

A second kiss was unnecessary. It would have even taken something away from the first and what would inevitably be the last.

A sense of unexplainable freedom flooded Adam's consciousness. They were finally free. He was free to go; she was free to let him. They had tried to get there the night before, but they needed the anger to go that deep. Finally, they were at peace with their relationship. At peace with their futures.

Adam wondered if maybe this was how God had planned it.

* * *

Sarge came through the door and Courtney pulled away. Adam didn't release his grip, instead he pulled her back toward him. Sarge saw them and started to leave, but Adam motioned for him to stay.

"Sarge, it's okay. Come here. I have something I want to tell both of you."

Sarge walked quickly over to them, grabbing a box of tissues off of the table.

They both wiped away the tears, and then Adam took Courtney back in his arms, and she rested her head on his shoulder. Adam pulled Sarge closer with his other arm. Sarge placed one arm around Adam and one around Courtney.

"Promise me something. Both of you. Okay."

They both nodded.

"Promise you what?" Courtney asked.

"Promise me you'll find Jamie when I'm gone."

"We *are* going to find her in time. She was only an hour away, and that was an hour ago," Sarge said.

"I know. I'm holding out hope too. But if she doesn't make it, promise me you'll find her. Tell her I'm sorry."

"Tell her that I didn't know about her. Courtney knows the whole story. Don't make her mother look bad. Just tell her that I didn't abandon her. If I had known, I would've been there for her. Tell her to forgive me."

Sarge wiped his eyes.

"Adam, she will forgive you. There's nothing to forgive you for. You didn't know," Courtney said in almost a whisper.

"Just promise me."

And they did.

* * *

A couple staffers appeared at the door. They were there to escort Adam to the reception and then to the launch pad. Sarge wrapped his arms around Adam and squeezed tightly.

"Hey, Sarge," Adam said. "When you get your next round of recruits, say something nice about me to them."

"I will if I can think of something."

They all laughed and Sarge laughed the hardest. He turned and walked out the door and motioned for the two staffers to join him.

Courtney said to Adam, "Always know that I love you, and I'm praying for you."

"We're taking the term 'long distance relationship' to a whole new level," Adam said.

Courtney laughed. Adam loved her laugh. He tried to etch it in his memory so he could draw on it over the next thousand years.

"I love you too."

Then he left.

Chapter Nine

C arl Brayton finished embedding the glitch into the software after agonizing for an hour over whether or not he should even do it. Adam's words resonated with him. *What if it was your daughter?*

Adam wanted him to sabotage the mission so he could talk to his daughter. Carl admitted to himself that if it was his daughter, he would want someone to do the same thing for him. It felt counter-intuitive, though. Most of the time, he built firewalls to prevent glitches. NASA had some of the most elaborate firewalls known to man, and Carl was one of the few people on earth who could maneuver his way around them.

He embedded a minor glitch that would take thirty minutes to fix, which meant if and when the light went on the mission would have to be scrubbed. He wasn't even sure he would activate it, but he'd have that option.

The glitch could only be activated by a password seventeen characters long. Once the glitch activated at precisely ten minutes to launch, the password had to be entered within one minute. If it wasn't, the glitch would self-destruct on its own. Under any other circumstances, this would be considered an ingenious plan.

The main concern was that the password had to be entered carefully. If one digit was wrongly entered, the glitch wouldn't activate the warning light but would create a software problem that could cause the spacecraft to veer out of control after launch. That had caused Carl to reconsider. *Is it worth the risk? What if I entered it wrong? I could put Adam's life in danger.*

"It should be all right," he reassured himself.

Why do I have an eerie feeling that it won't be?

* * *

2:52 p.m. 30 minutes to launch

Jamie had never laughed so hard in her life.

"What do two people from Alabama say after they break up?" Bud asked.

"I don't know. What?" Jamie asked.

"Let's just be cousins." Bud roared with laughter.

Jamie tried not to laugh too hard because her head hurt when she did, but she couldn't help it. Bud's jokes weren't that funny, but his delivery was cracking her up. She'd been leery at first getting into a truck with a total stranger. Bud was as harmless as a fly and a godsend. He had gotten her to within five miles of the exit to Kennedy Space Center, but they were now at a standstill. Traffic was backed up as far as they could see. They had moved less than a mile in the last forty-five minutes.

"This traffic is unbelievable," Jamie said sorrowfully. Her chances of making it to see her dad before his launch diminished with each second they sat there.

"It must be all the people coming out to watch the launch of that crazy person who's going off into space for a thousand years," Bud said.

Jamie fought back tears.

"What's the matter, sugar?" Bud hadn't said it improperly. It was said more like a grandfather talking to his granddaughter.

"Bud, I'm sorry." Jamie took a moment to try to compose herself. "I haven't been completely honest with you. My name is not Beth, it's Jamie. That crazy person going into space is my father. I was driving from Miami to the space center so I could talk to him one last time before the launch. My car ran out of gas, and I thought I wasn't going to make it. Then you came along and offered me a ride. You've been so great."

"Why didn't you say so? I might have been able to get you there in time."

Jamie hesitated.

"Because the police are looking for me, and I didn't want you to get in trouble," she let spill out.

"Why would the law be looking for you? What did you do?"

"I killed a guy at my hotel."

"What?" Bud's eyes widened and his mouth twisted in disbelief.

"He attacked me first. But I hit him really hard with my elbow, and I guess I killed him. They've been chasing me all day. I'm sorry, Bud. I should've told you."

"Sounds to me like it was self-defense." Bud didn't sound concerned at all.

"I've been trying so hard to get to the launch." Jamie's voice cracked and she began to cry. "All I wanted to do was talk to my dad one time before he left for a thousand years. Now, I'll never make it. The launch is at three o'clock. It's not your fault."

"The launch is not until three twenty-two."

Why would he say that? She was sure the news said three.

"It was delayed by twenty-two minutes," Bud explained. "I heard it on the radio back before I picked you up."

"Oh... I still don't think I can get there in time. This traffic isn't going anywhere anytime soon. I could start running, but it would take me an hour to get there. I don't even know if they would let me in the gate. I don't know what to do."

"I do," Bud said. "Hang on."

Bud turned the rig sharply to the right and accelerated, driving precariously on the shoulder. Jamie clutched the armrest in fear. Angry motorists honked as they passed by them. There was an exit just ahead but a bridge between them and the exit.

"You can't go that way," Jamie yelled. "There's a bridge there."

Bud didn't answer her. His eyes remained squarely on the road, and he wasn't slowing down.

Right before the bridge, he jerked the truck to the right and down the embankment of the median over to the frontage road. The truck bounced violently, and the left tires tilted slightly.

Good thing Jamie wore her seat belt, or she would've hit her head on the ceiling of the truck—the head that was finally feeling better from the concussion.

She could feel the rig sinking in the soft grass in the median, but the big truck powered its way through and onto the service road, tilting slightly on its left wheels again until it finally found its traction on the pavement.

"Where are you going?" Jamie asked anxiously.

"I hauled a big load of stuff to Kennedy Space Center a few months ago," Bud said. "It was a bunch of parts from somewhere. I don't remember. It doesn't matter. Anyway, they have a back entrance."

Jamie clapped her hands with excitement.

"If I can remember how to get there, I can get you to the gate. I'll tell them I have a load to drop off. With any luck, they'll let us in, and I'll drive you over to the launch building. I know which one it is. When I was there, the guy gave me a tour and told me where everything was."

"I could kiss you," Jamie said.

"You could, but I'm a happily married man." Bud grinned widely as he said it.

Bud drove like a maniac to the back gate. Jamie held on for dear life as Bud sped around each curve. They arrived in less than ten minutes. It was exactly three o'clock. The supply entrance was heavily guarded, and that side of the complex was surrounded by a large twelve-foot fence with barbed wire at the top. The entrance had a guard booth and a strong-arm traffic barrier that raised and lowered, probably by a control in the guardhouse.

The booth was manned by an older security guard with a protruding belly that rolled over his pants that were at least three sizes too small. He had a gun attached to his side. Jamie doubted he'd ever drawn it.

Bud eased the truck up to the entrance and said in his disarmingly friendly voice, "How's it going, partner? I have a delivery."

The security guard said, "This entrance is closed until one hour after the launch."

Jamie's heart sank.

The guard looked at his watch and said, "The launch is about to go. You can unload about an hour and twenty minutes from now."

Bud shook his head no and said in a determined voice, "These items are for the after-party for the bigwigs. They were supposed to get here yesterday, but I was delayed. There are going to be some pretty upset people if I don't get these items in there. I'm not going anywhere near the launch site. I just need to take these over to the dining hall so they can get everything prepared. Go ahead and let me through so that we don't both get in trouble."

Jamie had a little bit of hope.

"What is your name and company?"

Bud gave him a name that sounded like he'd just made it up. He confirmed it when he turned and winked at Jamie.

The guard looked down at the clipboard and said, "I don't see anything about any delivery."

"Like I said, it was for yesterday. It's probably not on today's schedule."

"My orders are to not let anybody through until after the launch."

"Is your supervisor here?" Bud said.

"No."

"Well, go call him. I don't think he's going to be very happy about the fact that you aren't letting us through."

"Hold tight for a moment."

The guard turned around and walked into the guardhouse. He picked up the phone and dialed a number. The other guards were watching them closely.

Bud turned to Jamie and said, "Hold on tight. We're going for a ride." He gunned the engine and smashed through the security arm, breaking it in half.

Jamie screamed.

The truck moved surprisingly fast for such a big rig, and they were well away from the security gate by the time the armed guards ran after them, waving their hands, yelling at the top of their lungs.

Looking in the side mirror, Jamie saw them raise their guns. She screamed again. "Bud, you had better hurry."

"Don't worry, honey. They can't hurt this truck."

Bud had already rounded the corner and was out of range and out of sight of the guards. And he was grinning like a mischievous kid.

"Bud, you are in so much trouble."

* * *

3:10 p.m. 12 minutes to launch

It had been thirty minutes since the last preparations were made and Adam had been strapped into his seat and the door ominously closed and sealed tight.

The last ten minutes had been boring for Adam. He had nothing to do at that point. The checklist was complete, and he'd spent the last thirty minutes going back and forth between thoughts of Jamie and thoughts of Courtney. The realization had hit him between the eyes, that Jamie wasn't coming, or if she was, she wasn't going to make it in time. Carl had to buy him some time.

Adam was snugly strapped into his seat, ready for a launch he hoped wasn't going to happen.

Sarah came on the radio and said, "Adam, are you done with the checklist?"

"I am. I've been done for fifteen minutes."

Years before, astronauts had a long procedure list they had to go through before launch. Now, everything was done by computer. He only had to concern himself with personal things, such as stowing his private belongings, making sure everything was battened down, and checking the controls. The most important thing to him had been the Bible from Courtney, which he'd carefully stowed near his bed.

"Hey Adam, why did the astronaut stop to eat?" Sarah asked.

The question stopped Adam in his tracks. Sarah didn't usually start the banter.

"Why?" Adam said.

"Because it was launch time."

Adam retorted, "Hey Sarah, I'm reading a book about antigravity. It's impossible to put down."

Sarah's laugh came through the com. He was surprised she was joking with him. When it was nearing time for launch, she was usually all business. He was the one who had always initiated the silly jokes. Sarah knew how difficult the day had been and that they hadn't found Jamie. This must obviously be her way of consoling Adam, knowing how hard it must be for him.

She has no idea.

He felt a twinge of guilt. Sarah had worked so hard to make sure this launch went smoothly. Carl was about to sabotage it, and it was his fault.

It can't be helped. Sorry.

His thoughts turned back to Courtney and he chuckled to himself as he remembered when she had joined the corny jokes game.

"Hey Adam, what do you call a crazy spaceman?" Courtney had said.

"What?"

"An Astro-nut."

A few days later, she told another one. "Adam, why did the astronaut see a psychiatrist?"

"Why?"

"Because he's a Luna-tic."

Adam appreciated Courtney's corny jokes now more than he had then. He realized looking back, how hard she was trying to get into his world. If only he'd let her in sooner. He'd told her a joke as well.

"How many psychiatrists does it take to change a light bulb?

"How many?" Courtney groaned.

"Only one, but the light bulb has to really want to change."

Courtney laughed, although she later admitted she'd heard that joke a thousand times. That was a fond memory of Courtney. She'd laughed like she'd heard it for the first time. He realized she started falling for him even back then. The signs were evident. He'd started falling for her a long time before as well.

Don't start crying.

Adam nervously watched the clock. The countdown was coming up on ten minutes to launch.

This had better work. I hope Carl comes through.

* * *

Adam had seen Carl right before he boarded. Many of the employees who worked closely with Adam stopped by the holding room to say goodbye. Carl didn't say anything in particular about the glitch, but he nodded reassuringly, leading Adam to believe he was going to help him.

At exactly ten minutes and fifteen seconds to launch, Adam said to Sarah, "Where does an astronaut park his spacecraft?"

Sarah didn't answer. For a moment, he panicked. He'd forgotten Mission Control went through one of their most important launch checklists at exactly ten minutes to launch.

What if she didn't answer? Would Carl still know to execute the glitch?

"Where does an astronaut park his spacecraft?" Sarah answered, to Adam's relief.

"At a parking meteor."

"Good one, Adam. That might be your best one yet."

Adam looked at the clock. It was exactly ten minutes to launch.

* * *

Carl heard the cue and went to work. All the higher-ups in NASA were on the same frequency and could hear the conversations between Sarah and Adam. They could even break into the channel in the event of an emergency. The understanding was that Sarah was the only one who would communicate directly with Adam unless there was a real emergency.

With two minutes to go in the countdown, the feed between Adam and Mission Control would go out to the area holding the press and to the viewing room where the family, friends, and dignitaries had gathered. There was a five second delay and someone was standing by with a kill switch if it was necessary. If the astronaut's life was in danger, no one wanted the world, and especially the family, listening to what could possibly be a horrific situation.

Carl pulled up the link to the software glitch and typed the password, nervously entering the numbers and taking the time to check each one to make sure they were accurate.

Carl had entered ten numbers when Kellie, one of his associates, came to his desk, stood next to him and said, "We're all going out for drinks afterward. Do you want to come?"

"What?" Carl looked up at her and said coldly, "What do you want?"

"Drinks... Earth to Carl. After Commander Lang is in the space stream, we're all going out to Fratellos to celebrate. Are you in?"

Carl said rather rudely, "Can't you see I'm in the middle of something?" He immediately regretted the exchange. Kellie was his most valuable employee.

"Sorry..." Kellie said angrily and skulked away.

I'll have to apologize later.

Carl looked down at the password and panic set in, "What number was I on? I don't remember."

He thought he had typed in eleven numbers. "Was it eleven or twelve? Or was it ten? It was definitely eleven."

He started typing in the rest of the password but stopped

"But what if I'm wrong? I think it was ten and not eleven."

One wrong number could be deadly to Adam. He had to be sure.

"What do I do?"

He decided to start over and frantically backspaced to the beginning. He looked at the clock and it said 00:09:15. He would have to enter seventeen numbers in fifteen seconds. That was certainly possible, but if he didn't get it done in time, it would be like getting a number wrong. It wasn't worth the risk. Carl clicked out of the program and sighed deeply.

I'm sorry Adam. I really am sorry. Please forgive me, buddy.

Chapter Ten

T Minus 00:05:23 seconds to launch

Yusaf walked into the armory and calmly opened the box to the missile. He carefully removed the launch tube from its case, checked one last time, and sat it back down on top of the box. He returned to his post. He still had time.

The large countdown clock to the right of the launch pad read five minutes left until launch. He had his own countdown clock. With one-minute left, he would bring the missile out of the armory. With thirty seconds to launch, he would insert the Battery Coolant Unit, known as a BCU, into the missile launcher. From that point, he would only have forty-five seconds to launch the missile or the coolant would run out. The missile would detonate long before that point.

Yusaf breathed deeply, trying to control his anticipation and enthusiasm. Patience was a key to his ultimate success. Timing was critical. A missile fired now would kill thousands of people in the blast radius. If he waited until the rocket ignited, tens of thousands would die and every building within two miles would be leveled. He looked around. No one was within several hundred yards of him. He was a trusted employee whom no one would ever suspect would be contemplating such an act.

The sequence of events about to unfold played once more in his head for at least the thousandth time.

With twenty seconds left in the countdown, the engines would roar to life. Patience would still be required. The engines wouldn't fully ignite until six seconds. When the clock struck zero, the fuel thrusters would release all of their power, and a huge fireball would emerge from the launch pad and begin thrusting the spacecraft upward. That was when he would shout his praise to Allah, fire the missile, and death would come to the infidels.

He regretted the secrecy. How much would he love to step in front of the cameras a minute before and announce to the world the greatness of Allah. The crowd would watch in horror if he could publicly aim the missile, shoot it into the spacecraft, and then rain terror down upon the horrified masses. A wishful pipe dream. They couldn't have any advance warning. Security was everywhere, and if he were seen, even with only a few seconds to firing left, he could still be stopped.

Imagining the great victory brought him an excessive deal of earthly pleasure. Picturing the devastation in his mind would have to be enough. He wouldn't live to see any of it.

The images were seared into his mind. He had imagined everything. The sights, smells, and sounds of destruction.

The missile would have a high-pitched squeal as it streaked low across the ground toward the launch pad. Those present would see the flash without time to process what it was. Millions would see it on television, and the replay would loop thousands of times for years to come.

Screaming... He could hear the screams. Pain. He could smell the burning flesh. Tens of thousands, dead. Most burned beyond recognition. He could see their badly charred faces. Those unfortunate enough to survive the blast, would die a slow and agonizing death as first responders would be overwhelmed and unable to care for everyone. He could hear their cries for help.

The buildings would be destroyed. Authorities would search for days for survivors in the chaos. They were unlikely to find any. The

Kennedy Space Center complex would soon look like the neighborhoods he grew up in that were destroyed by American bombs.

It would be a war zone. Devastation everywhere. Rubble.

Yusaf pictured with satisfaction dead bodies lying everywhere. Body bags strewn along the vast ocean of concrete. The Vice President of the United States and the First Lady would be dead. Their funerals broadcasted live around the world. He only wished the President would be among the dead, but this was better. Security would have been tighter. Snipers would have been on the roofs to kill him the moment he stepped out of the shadows. Allah decided who would be there and who would die. He would not question Allah's will and plan.

Fellow Muslims would no doubt be dancing in the streets all around the world. A great victory would be celebrated tonight and tomorrow across the globe. His brothers would praise him as the greatest of all warriors. The day would be memorialized, and the anniversary remembered. Perhaps other fellow warriors would be inspired to inflict more destruction on this date in the future.

Seventy-two virgins awaited him in paradise. He could feel their touch.

He could already feel the satisfaction to come in the brief seconds between the time he fired the missile, to when the fireball would consume everyone including himself.

They won't even know what hit them.

* * *

T Minus 00:05:14 to launch

Bud drove the truck up to an intersection with two options. They could turn left or right. He didn't remember which way to go.

Jamie looked at him and shrugged her shoulders. "Which way?"

"My momma always said, 'When in doubt, always do right.'"

Bud swung the truck wide so it wouldn't end up in the ditch and headed right, hoping he'd made the right choice.

In less than a mile, they rounded a curve, and NASA, in all of her glorious splendor, came into view. He'd definitely made the right choice.

Bud pointed at the launch pad. "That's where your dad is."

Jamie was in awe. She had no idea it was this large. A sense of pride overwhelmed her as she thought about her dad and the millions of people who were watching him.

Bud pointed to a building off in the distance and said to Jamie, "That's where you need to go. That's the Mission Control building. You can even see the sign."

"I need to go to the launch tower. That's where my dad will be."

"No. You can't go there. Have you ever seen a launch? When it goes off, there will be a lot of smoke and fire. Don't go anywhere near that area. He's already in the spacecraft. You can't get to him there. Go to the control room."

The road turned to acres of concrete as far as the eye could see. Bud steered the truck toward a large gate. A fence fully enclosing the section separated them from the area with the buildings. No guards were there, but the gate was closed.

Jamie looked in their rearview mirror and saw three cars racing toward them with their lights flashing. They were still a distance away.

She screamed, "Bud, you have to hurry!"

Bud drove the truck right up to the gate, turning the truck sideways. Jamie's side was out of view of the oncoming cars.

"Go!" he said emphatically. "Now. Run as fast as you can to that building. Can you get over that fence?"

Jamie nodded. She leaned over and kissed Bud on the cheek and said, "I'll never forget you."

"Run. They don't know you are here. Get over the fence and out of sight as quickly as you can so they don't see you. If they see you, they'll come after you."

Jamie jumped out of the cab and bounded over the fence as if it wasn't there. She sprinted what felt like a hundred plus yards and hid behind a large building. Bud's truck was quickly surrounded by armed troopers with their guns drawn. For a moment her eyes met Bud's, and he smiled briefly, obviously relieved she'd made it. He exited the truck with his hands in the air. The last she saw, he was lying face down, spread eagle, with the officers standing over him, their guns pointed at him.

They weren't looking her way at all.

Jamie took off running without looking back. She could do nothing for Bud now. His efforts would be wasted if she couldn't get to Mission Control in time. She had to make sure that didn't happen.

* * *

T Minus 00:02:14 to launch

Carl hadn't come through. After Adam cued Carl with the astronaut joke, several anxious minutes had passed, but the alarm never came on. Adam resigned himself to the fact that talking to Jamie wasn't going to happen. He felt a moment of resentment toward Carl but quickly put it out of his mind. It had been too much to ask of him anyway.

As the countdown hit two minutes, it occurred to him that maybe he could somehow get out of the spacecraft and set off his own alarm. He unbuckled his seat belts, flipped off the camera focused on him in the seat, and looked for a way to escape. The door was airtight shut. It could be opened from the inside, but it took several complicated steps. What would he do if he opened it? The spaceship was twenty stories high.

The countdown clock read exactly one minute to launch. Adam panicked as he realized he had less than thirty seconds to find a way to stop the mission. He looked around for any button that would alert Mission Control there was a problem but couldn't be traced back to him. No options came immediately to mind.

Thirty seconds later, the auxiliary power units turned on. Adam felt the power of the main engines lighting. Chronos 7 tilted forward for a moment and then rocked back. That was normal and would have been no big deal if Adam had been strapped in. Instead, he was knocked backward onto the floor.

The whole spacecraft rumbled and shook like a volcano getting ready to erupt. The powerful engines roared to life. The sound was so intense Adam could feel the vibrations in his chest. In less than twenty seconds, Adam would feel the full force of 3gs on his body, and he would be violently smashed against the wall and killed instantly. He imagined for a moment what Sarah and all of Mission Control would think when they tried to contact him, and he didn't answer. They would never know what happened.

Adam's life flashed before his eyes. The years of training were out the window. *Is this how the mission is going to end? Doomed before it ever started. How stupid am I?*

"What did you think you were going to do? Jump out of the spacecraft," he said to himself aloud. This wasn't a scripted action movie. This was real life, and he had screwed up big time. His emotions had gotten the best of him. His desire to talk to Jamie had put him in grave danger.

Adam fought against the forces of gravity and pent up thrust working against him. He tried to reach something he could use to pull himself up. The radio was too far away to warn Sarah. And the seat belts had no warning light to tell mission control the astronaut wasn't in his seat. No one ever contemplated a scenario in which someone would be stupid enough to unbuckle his seat restraints right at blast off.

Adam stayed off of his feet and crawled over to the seat. It took all his strength to pull himself up. The countdown reverberated in his ears. He turned with his back to the chair. His only chance was to fall backward as soon as the vehicle began to move and hope the

G forces kept him in his seat.

10, 9, 8...

I can't believe this is how I'm going to die.

* * *

The giant countdown clock showed the launch was less than two minutes away. Jamie estimated it would take her about two minutes to sprint to the building Bud had pointed at.

About halfway there, she caught a glimpse of something out of the corner of her eye. It was a man stepping out of the shadows of a building. He was holding some type of weapon on his shoulder. Terror came over Jamie as she realized it was a missile. She remembered seeing a report of terrorists shooting shoulder-fired missiles at airplanes. He was pointing it right at her dad's spacecraft.

He was more than thirty yards away, so she quickened her pace. He fumbled with something on the top of the weapon so she had a few seconds to get to him before he would be ready to fire.

I must stop him.

Her options were limited. She wanted to hit him high with a clothesline maneuver. That was the best way to disable him, but he had the weapon on his shoulder blocking her from hitting him in the head. Hitting him in the body was the best option.

Jamie launched herself like a missile, lowering her body, ducking her head, and hitting him like a linebacker would hit a running back.

They fell to the ground. The missile clanged noisily when it hit the ground and slid harmlessly away. Her head bounced off the concrete, sending pain ricocheting through her entire body. In a flash, he was on top of her. This wasn't Fletcher. He was strong, experienced. A scream formed in her throat, but his arm pressed into her neck cut off her ability to inhale enough air to let out the even weakest noise.

She tried to roll away, but he wrapped his muscular forearm around her neck from behind. A slight twist of her head kept him from getting a full grip. Her trainer had put her in this same hold many times before with just as strong of a grip. But it wasn't the same thing. This was real life. The trainer would loosen his grip when she tapped him on the arm letting him know she'd had enough. This man wasn't going to stop until she was dead. With the blood and oxygen supply cut off from her brain, it would be only a matter of seconds before she would lose consciousness. She had to get out of this on her own.

Jamie kicked his shin with her heel, delivering only a glancing blow. Hard enough only for him to move his legs and wrap them around her waist like scissors. That had been a mistake. Now his legs were like a boa constrictor slowly squeezing the life out of her. Every part of her body screamed in pain and demanded her attention.

She threw her head backward, trying to hit him with the back of her head.

He strengthened the grip, seeming to barely notice. He let out a huge breath as he squeezed harder.

Jamie struggled to catch even the slightest breath. Gasps were all she could muster. Her lungs burned from the lack of air.

She couldn't hold him off much longer. He was a fighter. A trained killer. A terrorist. She was a nineteen-year-old girl who practiced martial arts in a local gym. This would be over soon.

Elbows Jamie. Hit him with your elbow. You have to get off of the ground.

Jamie had long skinny arms with sharp elbows. They'd always been her best weapons in fighting. Her instructor had drilled in her to use them in a life and death situation.

That time had come.

She'd been pulling on his arm with her right arm to try and hold back the chokehold. It didn't stop him. She released it and twisted slightly to the left. She then flung her elbow to the right, connecting on his right side just below his shoulder. He grunted from the blow, but it caused him to only squeeze harder. It didn't faze him at all.

Jamie was going in and out of consciousness. She mustered what was left of her strength and twisted as far to the left as he would allow. She then flung her body back to the right and brought the sharpest part of her elbow into the side of his chest with as much force as she could muster. The sound of a rib cracking let her know that she'd hit her mark.

He loosened his grip as her elbow dug deep into his side.

He released his right arm and reached for his side. His left arm was still firmly around Jamie's neck, but the blow weakened it enough for her to wiggle free and jump to her feet. Her first instinct was to run, but the missile was still within his reach, and the spacecraft was still on the launch pad.

I have to stop him. He'll kill us all.

She tried to kick him in the groin, but it glanced off his thigh.

He grabbed the back of Jamie's leg, almost causing her to lose her balance and fall. He jumped to his feet as she barely kept hers. Before she could react, he slapped her across the face with the back of his hand.

She could taste blood.

He lunged for the missile.

She pushed him from behind.

Enraged, he turned back toward her. Their eyes met, and Jamie could feel the hatred searing from his cold, stone face.

At that exact moment, the earth began shaking violently. The spacecraft roared to life as the engines ignited, sending plumes of smoke cascading from the launch pad.

He turned and looked in that direction.

The words of Jamie's instructor resonated in her head. *Ignore distractions. Use them to your advantage.* Jamie needed this opening

He looked at the spacecraft and then at the missile on the ground.

Jamie shouted at the top of her lungs, trying to get his attention.

He turned back toward her. As he did, she balled her hand into a fist, raising the knuckle of her middle finger slightly. She timed it perfectly, bringing her right arm in a roundhouse arc, striking him with her knuckle at a spot slightly below his Adam's apple. Her knuckle penetrated the soft and vulnerable tissue, successfully crushing his vocal cords and trachea.

A fatal blow.

His face filled with fear. The hands and arms that seconds before were squeezing the life out of her, were raised to his neck as he gasped for air. The only thing that could have saved him would be a doctor skilled in opening a hole in his neck below the damaged trachea and then blowing air through a straw into his lungs.

Jamie swept his legs out from under him, and he fell backward onto the pavement, his head making a cracking sound as it banged off of the concrete.

I hope you have a concussion.

He thrashed around, desperately gasping for a breath that would never come. Gurgling sounds came from the back of his throat.

A concussion won't matter. He'll be dead soon.

Not wanting to watch him die, Jamie ran from the scene toward her original destination. She stopped only to watch her father's spacecraft soar into the atmosphere, leaving behind a trail of smoke and fire. She was in the open, but no one was looking at her. A scan of the crowd confirmed that everyone was looking in the sky. They were all fixated on the glorious spacecraft soaring rapidly into space.

I'm sorry, Dad. I did everything I could to get to you.

The thought occurred to Jamie that maybe God had brought her there to save everyone from the terrorist. Even though she hadn't arrived in time to see her dad, she had saved thousands of lives. That would have to be satisfaction enough.

I love you, Dad. I got to see your launch. I hope you are okay.

Chapter Eleven

"Chronos 7, Tower. Everything is looking good from here. Over."

Silence.

Sarah looked up from the launch data numbers she was perusing. Mission Control was making its first contact with Adam since the launch. He did not respond.

"Chronos 7, Tower. Trajectory is good. Thrust is good. Over."

The silence became deafening.

Sarah looked over at her ground flight commander, who shrugged his shoulders.

"Cut the outside feed for a moment," Sarah said.

She pushed a button on her computer. "Adam, is everything okay?"

No response.

"Is the video feed still off?" Sarah asked. The astronauts often turned it off before launch. They had complained that the images of them being hit by 3gs during launch was unflattering, and they preferred to have it turned off for the first minute. NASA had finally acquiesced.

"Yes. It's still off."

"Anyone seeing any problems?" Sarah asked. From her vantage point, the launch had gone perfectly.

"No. Everything looks good." That was the consensus around the room.

"Carl, is this a computer software problem?"

He paused before he answered. "I'm not aware of any problem. It could be a number of things, though. Perhaps a malfunction of the headset. It could be something as simple as a low battery."

"He could've passed out from the launch," one of the associates said.

"That's highly unlikely," Sarah explained. "Adam has been through this thousands of times in the simulator without a problem." Astronauts never passed out from a launch. Because of gravity, blood flows away from the head. A blackout would happen only if the blood flowed rapidly back to the head. That couldn't happen if the astronaut was in his chair.

"Is it instrumentation?" Sarah asked.

"There's no way of knowing. We aren't even seeing a problem here. How do we fix it, if we don't know what it is?"

"I wish he was connected to a monitor," Sarah said. In the distant past, NASA monitored the astronaut's vital signs through the entire flight. The astronauts had complained loudly about that as well. The men and women in the program maintained a high level of fitness. They felt it was unnecessary. Adam would only be in their range for one hour... totally unnecessary in his case.

"I agree. If we could see his vitals, we would know he's alive."

Sarah was silent for several seconds before she said, "Of course, he's alive. The launch went smoothly. Nothing traumatic happened that could've threatened his life. The oxygen levels in the cabin are good. From my seat, everything looks perfect. It looks like a very smooth ride."

"Do you want to abort?" the ground flight commander asked.

"Let's give it a few more minutes. Execute the roll and prepare for staging. We still have five minutes before we have to make that decision. If we don't hear from him by then, we'll have to consider it. In the meantime, keep trying to reach him and leave the outside feed off for now."

"What's going on, Adam? Are you okay?" Sarah mumbled under her breath.

Did you turn off your headset so I would abort... so you could talk to Jamie?

* * *

Jamie ran past the throng of reporters with adrenaline still coursing through her veins. They were snapping pictures at a rapid pace, at the wrong thing. Little did they know the young girl who'd been the focus of their obsession the entire day was running right in front of them. She bounded up the stairs and through a door marked "Authorized Personnel Only." A security guard was manning a table, but he had turned away from his post and was watching a television screen.

Jamie slipped past him and into the room. A large screen and several smaller TVs were showing live broadcasts of the launch. Several tables of food, drink, and water were in the back of the room. She headed directly to it and quickly downed several glasses of ice-cold water. Blood was coming from a scraped knee and elbow sustained while rolling around on the concrete. A wet napkin got rid of the blood. Her hands were still shaking from the confrontation with the terrorist. A deep breath calmed her slightly.

It felt like everything on her body hurt. Her head. The cuts and scrapes. Her neck was bruised from his arms compressing against it. Her sides ached from where his legs were crushing them from the powerful scissor hold. Thankfully, it didn't appear any ribs were broken. They were bruised, but it certainly could have been a lot worse.

She ignored the pain and made her way to the back of the viewing area intent on watching her dad's spacecraft on the large viewing screen.

A security guard walked toward her. Two others started moving toward her from a different direction. Soon she was surrounded by the three of them.

"You're not supposed to be in here," one said. "You need a pass."

Everyone had lanyards with NASA passes in them. A scan of the room confirmed to Jamie that she looked out of place in her shorts, tank top, and sneakers. Most were in dresses, or suits and ties.

"My name is Jamie Austen. I'm the astronaut's daughter," she said proudly.

"Right, and I'm the President of the United States."

Jamie stuck out her hand and said, "Hi, Mr. President, it's nice to meet you. You look taller on television."

"So, you're a wise guy." He grabbed her by the arm. "Come with me."

Jamie jerked her arm out of his grasp and said loudly, "Get your hands off of me."

* * *

Courtney sat in the front row of the viewing room. Senator Robinson, the Vice President, and the First Lady were sitting next to her. Adam insisted she stay for the launch and sit with the dignitaries. A commotion in the back of the room drew her attention away from the viewing screen.

Courtney threw her hands on her cheeks in amazement. She couldn't believe her eyes. Jamie was standing in the back of the room having some sort of confrontation with three security guards. It was, without a doubt, the girl in the video at the hotel. She rushed to the back of the room as things were getting more heated.

Courtney flashed her VIP lanyard at the security guards and said, "It's okay. She's with me." That seemed to satisfy them because they turned around and left but not before one of them gave Jamie a stern glare. She gave him one right back.

Courtney held out her hand and said, "Hi Jamie. My name is Courtney. I'm a good friend of your father. We've been looking all over for you."

"You wouldn't believe what I've been through trying to get here." Tears began to well up in her eyes. "I'm too late. My dad is gone. I wanted to talk to him."

"Did you see the press conference this morning?" Courtney asked.

"I did," she said, her shoulders sagging as she spoke.

"That's what we thought. You heard your name mentioned and left your hotel to come here to meet your dad."

"They mentioned my name?" Her eyes widened in surprise. "Why would they mention me at the press conference?"

"A reporter asked your dad a question about you. We thought you heard it."

"I didn't. I must have left before then. My dad knows about me?"

"He has known about you for a couple years."

"What? How could he? My mom said she never told him."

"He was at her funeral."

Jamie was quiet for a moment, clearly trying to process the new information. "He knew about me but never said anything?"

"He wanted to. He looked for you and desperately wanted to meet you. He's been searching all day. We all have." Courtney furrowed her eyebrows. Something Jamie said suddenly registered.

"Wait... If you didn't hear your name from the press conference, how did you know Adam is your father?"

"My mom told me right before she died. I promised her I would find him. I've been looking for him for two whole years."

Courtney pondered that for a moment. Adam had so many opportunities to talk to Jamie. *She knew all along and was even looking for him.* Adam was outside Jamie's dorm room two weeks ago. He could've talked to her then. Should have. *Oh Adam...*

Finally, Courtney said, "We can talk about that later. The main thing is that you're here. I need to get you over to Mission Control so you can talk to your dad."

"I can still talk to him?" she asked excitedly.

"Yes. We can connect you by a video hookup and you can talk directly to him. We must hurry though. In less than an hour, he'll go into the space stream."

Courtney saw the dignitaries starting to leave, including Senator Robinson. She yelled across the room for the Senator, got his attention, and motioned for him to come to where she was standing.

"Senator Robinson, I'd like you to meet Jamie Austen, Adam's daughter."

A huge smile came on his face. He held out his hand and said, "Young lady, you don't know how happy I am to meet you. You've caused me a lot of trouble today, trying to find you."

Jamie shook his hand, matching his smile. "I've never met a Senator before."

"We have a lot to tell you," Courtney said.

At that moment, two uniformed police officers walked through the door.

Jamie turned her back to them. "I have a lot to tell you too."

"There'll be plenty of time for that. Let's go talk to your dad," Courtney said.

* * *

"Chronos 7, Tower. Do you read me? Over."

Adam adjusted the volume on his headset.

He heard someone else say, "Sarah, are we going to abort?"

Adam was waiting anxiously for her answer.

"Standby," Sarah said. "I'm on the phone with Administrator Matthews discussing it right now. Get your procedures ready for an RTLS just in case. We will have a decision shortly."

An "RTLS" was a Return to Launch Site abort, a procedure put in place to abort a mission that had run into difficulty. It had never been attempted in the history of NASA and certainly wasn't without risk. An RTLS required what was called a "flip 'n burn." An unnatural act of physics. The spacecraft's trajectory was reversed, fuel burned off, and a burn executed to accelerate Adam back to earth with a shallow reentry. If all things went well, Adam would glide back into Cape Canaveral about twenty-five minutes after takeoff.

He'd barely survived takeoff. The upward thrust of liftoff had thrown him backward into his chair. The 3gs had pinned him to the chair like an elephant sitting on his chest. For the first few moments after launch, Adam was unable to move his arms. Just in time, he was able to get his shoulder harness around his upper body. That was the only thing that saved him. When the rocket pitched, he would have been violently thrown around the spacecraft and killed instantly if he hadn't been strapped in. As it was, he was pretty banged up but had no serious injuries.

When he heard the tower routinely calling for him, he got the idea not to answer. He calculated that they might consider aborting the mission altogether if they couldn't reach him. If they did an RTLS abort, he would return to the launch site, and he could continue his search for Jamie. Explaining why he didn't answer was problematic, but he would deal with that later.

Adam was certain that they would decide to abort. Administrator Matthews was very conservative and almost always erred on the side of caution. While an RTLS had risks, Adam couldn't imagine that NASA would send an unresponsive astronaut into space with no idea what had happened to him. The decision had to come in the next minute or they would miss the window of opportunity for an RTLS.

They could still decide on what was called an ATO, Abort to Orbit procedure, but Adam was hoping they didn't choose that option. If they did, he wouldn't return to Kennedy but would land somewhere off the coast of Africa. That would take several hours. He could never explain why he was without communications for that long. Technicians would discover that there were no mechanical problems. If they found that Adam had sabotaged the mission to that extent, he could be court-martialed and spend many years in jail.

This was the longest minute of Adam's life.

No answer came over the radio. Instead, the SRBs, Solid Rocket Boosters separated from the main spacecraft, and Chronos 7 was propelled out of earth's orbit. In a matter of a minute, he went from bright sunshine, to total darkness and sudden weightlessness.

His heart sank as his last hope to return to Kennedy was lost.

Adam reached over and engaged his headset.

"Tower. This is Chronos. I read you. Roger."

* * *

Carl Brayton heard the cheers when Adam's voice resounded over the intercom system. Adam had explained that he could hear the Tower's communications to him, but for some reason, they couldn't hear him. When the rocket separation occurred, something unexplainable happened, and they could suddenly hear him.

Carl was not one of the ones celebrating. He was praying ardently the mission would be aborted, and Adam would be returned safely to Kennedy. Carl knew something that no one else knew. Adam's life was in extreme danger.

After the launch, Carl went into the software to remove the glitch altogether. What he found sent shockwaves of terror through his whole body. The glitch had activated. "How's that possible?" He hadn't entered the wrong password. They were deleted before he finished entering them.

What he hadn't realized was that once he started entering the password, even though he didn't complete it, the system assumed the same result as entering the wrong password. *How could I have* been so stupid? Any initiation of the password set the software glitch in motion. Once he started, he had to finish for the glitch not to activate.

It could go off at any time.

If they didn't choose to abort, a disaster was looming. Carl had designed the glitch to send a false warning light that there was something wrong with the left flap. The warning light would not be a problem if the spacecraft was on the ground. It was a huge problem if the spacecraft was in the air.

At this point, the autopilot was flying the plane. When the warning light comes on, the autopilot wouldn't be able to tell if the light was real or not. It would assume it was and think it needed to correct the error. The left flap was actually in the correct position

It would then move the left flap from the correct position to the wrong position. That would cause the spacecraft to spin out of control. The autopilot would then try to correct, but its corrections would be based on an incorrect reading on the flap. Any correction would just make matters worse.

Carl could fix it, but it would take about thirty minutes. The problem was that the warning light could come on at any time. It could be up to an hour before it activated, or it could happen right then. He shuddered at the thought and got back to work.

Carl continued to work as fast as he could to fix the software. It would go a lot faster if he had another person to help. He looked across the room and saw Kellie, his associate whom he'd been rude to earlier. Now, he didn't even remember what she had asked him; he just remembered that he'd yelled at her, and she had been giving him cold looks ever since. He stopped what he was doing and walked over to her desk.

"Kellie, I need your help with something."

"Go away," she said coldly.

"Kellie, I'm serious. I found a software glitch that could jeopardize the mission."

She sat up in her chair.

"I don't know if it was a hacker or not, but we have to fix it before Commander Lang hits the space stream."

"What kind of glitch?"

"It will send a warning light that the left flap is out of position even though it's not."

She smacked the palm of her hand on her forehead. "That will send the spacecraft tumbling out of control."

"I know. We have to fix it and fast."

Kellie might be mad at him, but she was a professional above all else, and personal feelings never came before a mission. She might be suspicious about the glitch, but Carl doubted she could or would even try to prove it was him. Besides, saving Adam's life was way more important to him. If he lost his job over it, so be it. He wasn't going to put his career over Adam's life.

"Where is the glitch?

"It's in the steering system. At any time, a false warning light could come on indicating a problem with the left flap. I just discovered it by accident. That light will cause the autopilot to go crazy. I've been working on getting rid of the glitch altogether, but that's going to take time, and it could go off at any minute."

"Just turn off the warning light mechanism between the left flap and the autopilot," Kellie said. "The warning light might turn on, but if the autopilot doesn't know about it, it won't react. That should only take a few minutes. Then we can fix the glitch and get rid of it altogether. We'll need to reconnect the warning light after the software is fixed. Commander Lang might need it later."

"Kellie, you are a genius. Can you fix that for me right away, and I'll keep working on fixing the glitch?"

"I'm on it."

Carl felt better. But not much.

Chapter Twelve

Sarah decided not to tell Adam right away that Jamie was there. It would be ten minutes before she was in the room with the video hookup, and she wanted to get the checklist for the space stream entry completed early so Adam would have plenty of time to talk to her.

"Adam, I want to go ahead and go through our entry procedures now." The protocol was to go over them twenty minutes before entry.

"Why now? You got somewhere you have to be?" Adam said.

She laughed. "I would like to go home early today."

"Do you have a hot date? Not very considerate of you to make plans on my launch day," Adam said.

Going home early was not going to happen. NASA was abuzz about word of a security guard who was killed, and a shoulder fired missile that had been discovered next to his body. Everything was on lock down as they searched the grounds for a potential terrorist who had killed the security guard. Also, details were sketchy, but a truck had crashed through the supply gate shortly before launch and a man was in custody. They weren't sure if the two incidents were related. Administrator Matthews was dealing with those issues and had decided they shouldn't tell Adam.

Today was going to be a long day for Sarah. With normal space flights, she would be on the clock for several days until the astronauts got home safely. She had spent many nights on a bed in her office. That wasn't necessary on this flight. Once Adam was in the space stream, there was nothing more that she could do.

She was so excited to tell Adam about Jamie she couldn't wait.

"Adam, actually I want to do the procedures because we have a surprise for you."

"I'm not really in the mood for surprises." He started to say something else and then stopped mid sentence. "You mean..."

"Yes. That's the surprise. Jamie is here."

"She's there? She's with you?"

"She's not with me, but she's here. She saw the launch. You were right. She was coming to see you all along. They're getting everything set up now. We're going to put her on a video feed, and the two of you will have about thirty minutes to talk. I want to get these procedures done now so we don't have to cut short your time with her."

They finished the procedures in no time at all.

* * *

Talking to Jamie was nothing like Adam had envisioned it would be. At first it was awkward. She kept the promise to her mom. He explained things. Then it just flowed easily. Probably better than most conversations between fathers and teenage daughters in college. There was no history, no pretense, not enough time to waste words.

"What are you studying in college?"

"Why did you become an astronaut?"

"Any boyfriends?"

"I never remarried."

"What do you want to do when you get out of college?"

"Are you excited about what you might find in space?"

The conversation took an uncomfortable turn for Adam when Jamie said, "I think Courtney might be smitten with you."

She was staring at him, clearly looking for a reaction. Adam turned slightly red.

"I never stopped loving your mother," he said.

"I know... It's okay. I like Courtney."

"She's been a good friend to me. I hope you two become friends as well."

"She invited me to stay at her house tonight. She's so sweet."

"You should do that. But don't believe any of the things she says about me. They aren't true. Well, some of them are... Okay... All of them are."

"She said she gave you a Bible and you promised to read it."

"It's right beside my bed."

"I'm a Christian too. Promise me you'll read it."

"I already promised Courtney."

"I know, but if you promise both of us, then you'll definitely have to do it."

"After we get off the phone, I will put my hand on the Bible and swear."

"Don't do that. Put your hand on the Bible and open it."

"I promise. The two of you are already ganging up on me."

They had many questions for each other, and they were coming rapid fire. The answers were short, so they could ask more. He was filling the void in her quickly. She was everything, and more, he'd hoped she would be.

"I have an idea," Jamie said.

"What?" Adam couldn't stop grinning.

"Maybe I'll become an astronaut. I'll come find you in space."

"That's a great idea. You can use me as a reference. You already know Sarah and Courtney. They'll give you a reference as well. Get your degree. Join the program, and we'll have a family reunion on Kepler in a thousand years."

"Also, I can make sure you kept your promise to read the Bible. Leave me a trail of breadcrumbs, like Hansel and Gretel, on each planet along the way so I can find you."

They both laughed heartily. Years of pent up tension disappeared with each passing minute.

A large bang sounded inside the ship. The spacecraft lurched violently to the left and startled Adam.

Jamie screamed as she watched Adam being thrown from side to side.

He was being held in his chair only by his lap restraint.

Spinning... Shaking.

The camera captured every moment of horror.

Adam blacked out.

* * *

Jamie instinctively reached her hand to the screen, unable to reach him. She screamed louder as Courtney raced into the room. Courtney took one look at the screen and then looked away. She took Jamie in her arms and shielded her from the images of Adam being thrown around like a rag doll. Mercifully, the screen went black.

* * *

Alarms were going off all over mission control. The video and audio feeds had been turned off so that Adam and Jamie would have privacy. They were quickly turned back on.

"Are these real or false alarms?" Sarah shouted above the din.

No one answered because no one knew.

"Are they real or are they false alarms?" Sarah yelled at the top of her lungs.

Arnold, Sarah's Assistant Flight Director, said, "Look at the trajectory. Chronos is spinning out of control. It has to be real. We're going to have to correct this quickly, or Adam is going to tumble off into space."

Sarah watched in utter disbelief as she saw Adam being thrown from side to side like he was on a roller coaster. The autopilot had stopped the spinning, but it was overcorrecting and causing the craft to serpentine back and forth.

"Adam can you hear me?" Sarah asked. "What happened? What are you seeing?"

Adam sat unconscious in his seat.

"Carl, can you hear me?"

"I'm here, Sarah."

"Do you know anything about this?"

"We've found the problem, and we're trying to correct it now."

"How long is that going to take?"

"About three minutes. It's a false warning light, but the autopilot thinks it's real. We're turning off the link between the light and the autopilot. That should fix it momentarily. Kellie is working on that now."

"I don't think we have three minutes," Sarah said. "If this isn't corrected right away, Chronos is going to be so off course, Adam will never make the window in time. If he misses the entry, we may not be able to get him back. If the shaking continues, the spacecraft could break apart."

"We'll fix it as fast as we can."

Sarah said to Adam, "We're working on it now. It's going to take three minutes to fix. Are you okay for three minutes?" She had no idea if he could hear what she was saying, but she wanted to reassure him if she could.

Then she had an idea. "Can't we just turn the autopilot off?"

"Yes," Carl answered. "That will stop the problem momentarily, but Adam will have to steer manually. We'll still have to get it fixed. Adam can't steer manually twenty-four hours a day for a thousand years."

"He can't steer. He blacked out."

"Turn it off anyway," Carl advised. "We can steer it from here."

Sarah said to Arnold, "Turn off the autopilot. Get ready to manually steer."

A voice boomed on the intercom, "Flight, get ready to fly the spacecraft from here. I'm going to turn off the autopilot. That'll stop the erratic movements."

One of the other engineers said, "Sarah, you know there's a three second delay. Whatever moves we make here will take a few seconds to reach Chronos."

"I know, but factor that in your movements. It's better than what we have now. We have to bring the spacecraft under control."

"Are you ready?" Sarah was amazingly calm as she looked around the room. "Turn off the autopilot now. I hope this works."

She looked at the screen. The spaceship jolted when the autopilot was first turned off, and for a moment, it leveled off. Then it began to wobble and started to roll.

Sarah yelled, "The spacecraft is rolling! Stop the roll, now!"

The sudden jolt woke Adam. He opened his eyes, and said groggily, "Jamie are you still there?"

"Adam this is Sarah. Can you hear me? Are you okay?"

"I'm okay. What happened?"

Flight had stopped the roll momentarily.

"You blacked out for a moment," Sarah told him. "We've switched off the autopilot. We are having a hard time controlling it here. Are you okay to fly the spacecraft?"

It seemed to Sarah like Adam was starting to get his bearings. He looked at his control panel, appearing to be assessing the damage.

"Sarah, the warning light for steering just went off."

"That's good. Carl has been working on it. That was causing the problem. There was a software glitch. We're going to reset the whole system, but we can't do that until the computer glitch is fixed.

I don't want to turn the autopilot back on until I'm sure it's fixed. I don't want you going through that again."

* * *

"I'm taking control of the spacecraft now," Adam told Sarah. "I can fly it."

Was this whole mess my fault?

He'd told Carl to sabotage the system, and apparently, he had, but it didn't go as planned. What a disaster this had become. He was lucky his insides weren't splattered on the side of the wall when he took his seat belts off at launch. Now he was lucky he wasn't spinning uncontrollably out into space. All of it was for nothing anyway.

Jamie had made it in time. He got to talk to his daughter. If he got this problem solved, he could talk to her again. He had to put that out of his mind because he had work to do. One thing about Adam; he lived in the moment. At that moment, he had a spacecraft to fly. His life and the mission depended on it.

He would have a thousand years to kick himself.

* * *

Courtney said to Jamie, "What happened?"

Jamie said, "We were talking, and the spacecraft just went crazy. Is my dad going to be okay?"

"I don't know," she replied. Courtney didn't want to lie to her. "The best people in the world are working on it right now. Let me get you some water. Let's stay right here. When they get the problem fixed, I'm sure your dad is going to want to finish your conversation."

"Please tell me he's going to be okay," Jamie implored Courtney as she handed her the glass.

Courtney put her arms around Jamie and held her close. She stroked Jamie's head. "He's going to be okay."

"Do you mind if we say a quick prayer?"

I love this girl. Courtney led them in a prayer, and it seemed like it helped them both to feel better.

A man with a NASA ID tag walked in. "Everything is under control. Commander Lang is okay. There was a problem with the steering. They're working on it. We'll reestablish the feed with you as soon as possible. Just stand by, and we'll turn on the feed as soon as we can."

They thanked the man and then both thanked God at the same time.

"If my dad wasn't okay, would they tell us?" Jamie asked.

"Yes. They would. NASA has a policy to always be straightforward with loved ones. That way they can count on getting accurate information."

Jamie had abruptly turned her head when Courtney said, "loved ones." *I wonder if she knows we're more than friends.*

"I'm so glad you're here with me," Jamie said.

Courtney was still shaken. She simply couldn't let Jamie know it.

* * *

Adam was able to bring Chronos back under control and was flying it smoothly like a boat on a peaceful lake. He got the go ahead to switch the autopilot back on, which he did gladly.

He clicked on his headset and said, "Sarah, how far off course are we? Are we going to make our window?"

"We're looking at that now. We'll enter the corrections here, and all you have to do is sit back and enjoy the ride. Sorry, the ride hasn't been so good up to now. Are you holding up okay?"

"I'm good. Are we going to be able to get this fixed in time for me to talk to Jamie for a few more minutes?" Adam looked at the clock, and he had about twenty minutes before entry into the space stream.

"That's the plan. We're turning it on right now."

The television screen came back to life. Jamie was looking directly at the screen with anticipation.

"Sorry about that," he joked. "I dropped the call. I don't have very good cell phone service up here. I'm calling my telephone company first thing Monday morning."

"Be prepared to be on hold for a long time," Jamie said.

"I can be on hold for a thousand years. That might help me pass the time."

Then Adam unexpectedly saw Courtney's image on the screen next to Jamie's. "Hi. Courtney," he said lovingly.

Courtney said hello then stood to leave the room.

"No." Jamie grabbed her hand. "Stay with us. It's okay."

For fifteen minutes, Adam, Courtney, and Jamie talked nonstop. They could barely catch their breaths. They talked about so many things. Adam thought that it couldn't have been better if it were scripted. *These are the two most important people in the world to me.*

Jamie asked if they could all pray together before signing off.

Adam said he would like that.

Jamie prayed, "Father, thank you for my dad. Thank you for letting us have this time together. Be with him on this journey. Keep him safe in your arms. I pray that he will feel your presence with him every day. I pray that he will see Jesus."

"Thank you. That was a beautiful prayer," Adam said earnestly, and Courtney nodded in agreement.

"I love you," were the last words he said and the last words he heard from both ladies. And then the screen went blank.

* * *

At two minutes to entry, Carl had fixed the glitch; the autopilot was back on; and the course had been corrected. Adam did a quick check of the spacecraft and found nothing wrong other than a few broken things inside the ship. He couldn't inspect the outside; he would just have to assume that everything was okay. Nothing he could do about it now anyway.

Adam was amazingly calm. He'd spoken to Jamie, and he was at peace. He'd told Courtney he loved her, and he would take her love with him into his future, whatever it may be. Whatever happened in the entry would happen; he was resigned to his fate either way. He would always remember the last look he and Courtney had shared. He would always remember his last moments with Jamie.

Sarah's voice came on the intercom one last time. "Commander, are you ready for this?"

"No. I think I changed my mind. I've decided I don't want to go. Can you send someone else? Can you make sure I splash down near the Cayman Islands? I need a vacation."

"Hey Adam, why are there not any women astronauts on the moon?"

"Why Sarah?"

"Because it doesn't need cleaning yet."

Adam laughed and said, "I'm glad I didn't tell that joke. That's very sexist."

"Seriously, we're very proud of you here. Of all my pilots, you're the best one by far."

"I'm sure you say that to all your astronauts. Hey Sarah, what do you say to a clumsy astronaut?"

"What Adam?" Sarah said, fighting back the tears.

"Have a good trip."

"Have a good trip, Adam," Sarah said.

Ten seconds later, all the screens in Mission Control went blank as they lost contact with Chronos 7 and Adam entered the space stream. An eerie silence permeated the room. No one was cheering. No one was celebrating. No popping champagne corks. Only a somber respect for the moment. They had all done their jobs. They got Adam to the entry point. The rest was up to him.

He was in God's hands now.

Chapter Thirteen

Courtney and Jamie returned to the NASA conference room, fully satisfied with the conversation with Adam, considering the circumstances. Jamie was starving so she helped herself to the cold sandwiches, chips, dips, and vegetables waiting for them.

Courtney poured herself a soft drink, and they sat down in the luxurious chairs.

Nothing was said as Jamie scarfed down the food and went back for seconds. Courtney couldn't help but think about Adam, wondering if he survived the entry into the space stream.

"You're thinking about Dad, aren't you?" Jamie said, interrupting Courtney's thoughts.

Courtney nodded.

"You two were very close, weren't you?"

Courtney looked away and didn't answer but nodded.

"Do you think he survived the entry?"

"I'm sure of it," Courtney said emphatically.

"How can you be so sure?"

"Because that's the only way I can think of him. Alive. Happy. Resilient. I can't picture him any other way. Since I don't know for sure, I'm just going to trust God and believe that Adam is in his hands." Courtney said it with such affection she felt herself blushing.

Jamie looked away, clearly thinking.

Courtney noticed that was the same kind of thing her father did when he was suppressing his feelings.

She sensed what Jamie might be thinking and said, "Your father and I were just good friends. Nothing ever happened between us. He loved your mom. I don't think he ever got over her."

"She never got over him," Jamie said as she ran her fingers through her still-mussed hair. "Mom never remarried either. I wonder why neither of them ever married again. Anyway... it's okay, Courtney. I don't mind that you and my dad were close. I like you. And my dad likes you as well. I can tell. I think he was in love with you. I'm glad he had someone."

Jamie saying Adam was in love with her sent chills down Courtney's spine. She tried to change the subject, turning the conversation back to Adam and her mother. "They were young and just didn't know how to make things work at the time. If Adam had known about you, he never would have agreed to the divorce. Once he did learn about you, his whole perspective changed. He desperately wanted to know you."

"The way that happened... I think that really bothered my mom all the way until she died."

"I'm sorry about your mom."

Jamie didn't respond.

Courtney could tell Jamie had her own wounds. She didn't probe any further.

She changed the subject again. "What happened in Miami?"

"What about Miami?" Jamie looked down, darting her eyes from side to side.

She's hiding something. As a trained psychologist, Courtney was keenly aware of the signs of deception.

"The parking garage at the hotel. You made a 911 call, something about a woman being attacked."

Jamie hesitated. Probably calculating how much she should tell Courtney.

"It's okay. You can talk to me."

Finally, Jamie blurted out the whole story. The press conference, the note for her roommate, the parking garage, Fletcher. She told in detail how he followed her into the garage and then attacked her. He had a knife, then was on top of her and was going to kill her. She killed him first.

"You didn't kill him," Courtney told her. "He's still alive. He's in ICU, but he's going to live."

"Oh, thank God." Jamie let out a huge breath, clearly relieved. "I thought he was dead. Policemen and FBI men have been following me ever since I left Miami. They almost caught me, but I managed to escape."

Jamie explained how she kicked an FBI agent in the stomach, got away from him, and another man chased her and tried to get in her car.

Courtney thought the stories sounded like an action movie.

About that time, Senator Robinson walked in and sat down at the table next to them.

"That man you kicked wasn't FBI," he said, obviously having heard the last part of the conversation. "He was one of our men. He was NSA. I sent him there to try and find you."

Jamie threw her hands in the air. "Oh, for heaven's sake! I thought they were looking for me because I killed Fletcher."

"Fletcher's not dead. He's just beaten up pretty badly," the Senator explained.

"She knows. I told her," Courtney said.

"The Miami police don't know it was you in the garage. We changed the records so they couldn't trace it to you. From what you're saying, it was self-defense anyway."

"You mean no one is trying to arrest me?"

"No," he laughed. "No one is trying to arrest you. But what really happened in the garage? No one can figure it out."

Jamie quickly told the Senator the story.

Courtney was just as amazed the second time she heard it.

"So, you took down a three-hundred-pound man all by yourself and put him in intensive care," the Senator said. "Then you managed to beat up one of my trained men and escape another. Plus, you eluded the NSA and all our men who have been looking for you. Remind me not to get on your bad side. If you ever want a career as a spy, let me know, sounds like you would be a good one."

"By the way," the Senator added, "How did you get into the space center undetected?"

Jamie's eyes got as big as saucers.

"What?" Courtney said.

"Bud!" Jamie said, "I forgot about Bud."

"Who's Bud?" Courtney asked.

The Senator answered for her. "Bud is a trucker who crashed his rig through the back gate. He's being interrogated right now. The local police are about to arrest him and haul him to jail."

Jamie interjected hastily, "They can't do that. Bud was just helping me. It's my fault. I'm the one who should be arrested. Bud gave me a ride when my car broke down. You can't arrest him. Please... He's the sweetest man I've ever met. He went to the back gate, and the guards wouldn't let us in. That's why Bud smashed his truck through the gate—so I could see my dad. I hopped the fence and then ran over here."

Senator Robinson nodded as if finally understood what happened. "That had everyone perplexed. They thought it might be a terrorist attack or something."

Jamie laughed, "Bud a terrorist? He was in the army. He's as patriotic as it gets. Bud's nothing but a good old boy from Alabama."

"That's what they thought as well. They've been interrogating him over at the local FBI office for several hours. He won't talk. He won't tell them why he rammed the gate or what he was doing at Kennedy. They searched his truck, and all they found was a bunch of Chinese products that were scheduled to be delivered tomorrow in Baltimore. They thought he might have a bomb, but they couldn't even find any weapons in the truck."

"Is he in a lot of trouble?" Jamie asked nervously.

"He is, or he was." the Senator explained. "They have all kinds of charges they could bring against him, but they really didn't know what to do. He doesn't have a record. He has a nice family and kids. He showed our men pictures of his wife and kids. Like you said, he's as nice as he can be. But he wouldn't say why he was at Kennedy, so they couldn't let him go."

Senator Robinson pulled out his phone. "Now we know the story. He must like you. He wasn't going to give you up for anything. They let him make a phone call to his wife. We listened in on the conversation, but he didn't say anything incriminating. His wife was mad as a pig without food. She was also dumbfounded. Our men questioned her over the phone, and she couldn't shed any light as to why her husband would crash his truck into the Kennedy Space Center. I'm telling you; this was the most confusing thing our men had ever seen. Nobody ever thought it might be related to you."

"Is there anything you can do for him?" Courtney asked.

Senator Robinson dialed a number. "Thelma, patch me through to the guys who are interrogating that trucker down at the FBI office at Cape Canaveral. I'll hold."

"This is Senator Robinson. I am over at Kennedy in the conference room in Building D. That guy you are questioning, Bud, I want you to bring him over here as soon as possible. Tell the local authorities that we are taking it from here."

"No, we are not going to press charges against him." The Senator paused. "I don't care what the local authorities say. Tell them this is a federal matter. It was on government property, and they have no jurisdiction. Also, when you bring him over here, don't put any handcuffs on him. I know what happened, and I have sorted all of this out. Also, find out where his truck is. If it hasn't been towed, then leave it where it is. If it has been towed, tell them not to do anything with it. After you bring Bud here, you will need to take him to get his truck."

The Senator hung up the phone and looked very seriously at Jamie. "Young lady."

Jamie skulked back like a kid caught with her hand in the candy jar.

"You wouldn't happen to know anything about a dead security guard and a terrorist attack, would you?"

Courtney looked at Jamie with complete puzzlement on her face. This was the first she had heard about it. Jamie was looking away, fidgeting, tight lipped, and with a sly grin on her face. *She looks just like her dad. He had that same look sometimes.*

Jamie started talking slowly and then sped up to a pace that was barely understandable.

"It was horrible. After Bud rammed the truck through the gate, these men were chasing us with guns drawn. I jumped over the fence. I was trying to get over to Mission Control so I could find someone to let me talk to my dad." She paused long enough for a quick breath.

"Then I saw that guy wearing a security guard uniform, and he had a missile on his shoulder. He was pointing it straight at my dad!"

"Slow down for a minute." Senator Robinson was trying to calm her down.

"Are you saying that the security guard was the one holding the missile?"

"Yes. He was trying to kill my dad. If I hadn't come along, he would have."

"That missile would have killed your dad and every one of us," the Senator said with relief in his voice.

Courtney couldn't believe the story unfolding before her.

"What happened when you saw him with the missile?" the Senator asked.

Jamie started talking fast again. "I jumped on him. Then he got me in a chokehold. I thought he was going to kill me. I kicked him. I tried to hit him, but he was too strong. I elbowed him in the ribs, and I jumped to my feet. He went for the missile. I pushed him, and he slapped me on the face." She reached up and touched a mark above her lip. It was still red.

"You must have been petrified," Courtney said.

"I was. When he turned around, I hit him in the throat. Then I pushed him on the ground and started running over here. I knew he was dead. Did I do something wrong?"

"No, my dear, you saved the United States of America from a great tragedy."

"Really? I could tell he wanted to kill my dad. I didn't really think about it. I just reacted."

Courtney looked at Jamie in amazement.

The Senator picked up a phone and dialed another number. "Cancel the lock down and call off the search. I found out what happened with the security guard. He was the terrorist."

The Senator nodded his head toward Jamie. "Yes. I know who took him down. She's sitting right here next to me." He paused. "Yes. You heard me right. I said she. She is the one who killed him. Proud of her. She's an American hero. I'm going to see that she gets a medal."

At that time, Peter and Cathy, the Senator's aides walked in. He disconnected the call and had immediate instructions for them.

"Peter, find Jamie's Jeep. Return it to the Miami rental car center. Cathy, get Jamie a car up here and put it on my bill. Book her a suite at the finest hotel in this area."

"I'm staying with Courtney tonight," Jamie interrupted.

Courtney nodded enthusiastically.

"Okay. Scratch the hotel. But get her a car. Also, get a NASA physician over here right now to check her out. I want to make sure she doesn't have any serious injuries. Cathy, give Jamie your cell phone number. I want you to roll the red carpet out for this lady over the next few days. Whatever she wants or needs, you take care of her. Set up a meeting for her at the White House sometime next week." Turning his focus back to Jamie he said, "I want the President to meet you."

"I don't know what to say." Jamie said bashfully.

Courtney wondered if peanut butter sandwiches and macaroni and cheese were her favorite foods as well.

Courtney smiled at Jamie and felt a great sense of admiration. "She is just like her dad. Courageous. Resilient. Confident. Smart..."

He would be so proud of you right now.

* * *

Later that night, Courtney and Jamie were sitting on the deck at Courtney's house. Courtney was having iced tea, Jamie a soda. They were trying to unwind from the most eventful day in either of their lives.

Senator Robinson had managed to make sure Bud was not charged with anything and that he got his truck back. The Senator felt as though Bud had done his country a great service and deserved a medal, not charges. Bud was sworn to secrecy, but they all figured he might tell a few friends in a local watering hole over a few beers. No one would believe him, and no real harm could come of it.

When Jamie saw Bud, she ran across the room and threw her arms around his neck. He was still a little nervous, as the seriousness of what he'd done set in. He was relieved to see Jamie and more relieved when he was told that no charges would be filed, and that he was free to go with their thanks.

Jamie became emotional when she had to say goodbye to him.

Sarah and Administrator Matthews came by a little later and met Jamie, exchanged pleasantries, and wished her well. They spoke highly of her father. Jamie was even more impressed with her dad with each passing moment. They shared some funny stories about Adam and had a few laughs until it was time for everyone to go home.

Jamie called Rebecca and let her know everything was okay. She asked her to gather up her things and bring them back to George Mason. Courtney told Jamie they were going to go clothes shopping tomorrow. Not too early though. They were going to sleep in.

Senator Robinson took care of Jamie's Jeep that was at the impound lot. He had it picked up and taken back to Miami and turned in. Jamie didn't know who paid the towing or impound fee or the final charges. No one ever said anything. She figured it would be Senator Robinson.

The NASA doctor confirmed Jamie had a concussion, along with bruised ribs, a sprained wrist, several bumps and scrapes, a swollen knuckle, and several internal bruises. The doctor wanted her to go to the hospital and stay overnight for observation. Jamie insisted that she was fine, confirming to Courtney another way in which she was just like her dad.

Sitting on Courtney's deck restored peace to her weary soul. A welcomed reprieve to an eventful day. Her home was off the beaten path overlooking a lake. A modest house with three bedrooms, two baths, and a one car garage—typical for a single woman with no kids.

"What are you going to do now that you're going to be famous?" Courtney said half-jokingly. The news reporters had the full story of Jamie taking down the terrorist.

Jamie laughed. "My dad thinks I should be an astronaut. I told him I would come to Kepler and find him."

"A lot of people would give you a good reference. It helps that your dad is the most famous person in America. Actually, you might be." They both chuckled like they were not sure it was a good thing. Fortunately, the press knew nothing about Courtney, so Jamie could hide out at her house without the press hounding her.

"Senator Robinson said I should be a spy. I like the sound of that."

Courtney started to ask Jamie how she could possibly take down a three-hundred-pound man and a terrorist, but she stopped herself. *Why make her relive that all over again? She's just starting to relax.* Instead, she said, "You would make a good one."

Courtney looked at Jamie and noticed how beautiful she was in person. Jamie had taken a shower and was wearing a pair of Courtney's pajama bottoms and the T-shirt she'd purchased for her dad that read on the front, Life Would Be Boring Without Me.

"Do you think my dad is a Christian?" Jamie asked.

"I don't think so, but he is searching. I'm praying that he finds God on this journey."

Jamie shared how she grew up in church. Her mother insisted on taking her almost every Sunday. She was saved at a Vacation Bible School when she was ten-years old.

Courtney related that she was saved at a revival when she was seventeen.

Jamie said that she was considering joining a summer mission's program for college students. They were going to Haiti, and she might go.

Courtney said she should. They talked for several more hours about God, Adam, boys, and life in general. They really hit it off. Courtney wondered if they would stay in touch; she liked Jamie a lot.

She went inside for a moment, and when she returned, she handed Jamie an envelope.

"What is this?"

"Open it. It's a gift to you from your father."

It had the check Adam had given to Courtney the night before around the same spot on the deck.

At first, Jamie didn't seem to know what she was looking at.

"Your Dad gave it to me last night. He wanted you to have it."

"It's made out to you."

"He told me to find you and give it to you."

Jamie's eyes narrowed in disbelief. For a moment, she couldn't find words to say. "I can't believe this. This is so much money. I didn't know how I was going to pay for school next year. Mom didn't leave me with any money. I've been paying for it myself through student loans, but I can pay them off now."

"That was everything he owned on this earth, and he wanted me to find you and give it to you."

Jamie fought back tears. "He didn't even know me, and yet he was thinking of me."

Courtney nodded yes. "He loved you. Even though he didn't know you. You were his daughter. That meant something to him."

"This means so much to me, Dad," she said looking up at the stars.

Courtney followed her gaze. There were millions of stars radiating in the sky.

"It was nice of God to give us such a clear sky tonight of all nights."

"Dad, can you see the same stars we're seeing?" Jamie whispered.

Courtney stood and motioned for Jamie to follow her. They stood at the edge of the deck. "Do you see that big star up in the sky?" Courtney pointed, and Jamie moved closer to look directly at where she was pointing. Millions of stars dotted the night sky, but Jamie shook her head yes anyway.

"I think that's your Dad's spaceship right there."

"I think you're right!" Jamie said. "That looks like it, doesn't it?"

They grinned at each other, hugged, and sat back down.

They were both quiet for several minutes. Neither had any more tears left to shed.

PART TWO

"All journeys have secret destinations of which the traveler is unaware." *-Martin Buber*

Chapter Fourteen

300 years later

In the beginning, God created the heavens and the earth... and presumably Kepler 452b. The heavens and the earth were still there. Kepler was not.

* * *

Nothing I could say would make any sense. Last night when I went to bed, Kepler was there. This morning when I woke up, it wasn't. How do I explain that?

The video camera had been set up for several hours, but I'd been unable to find the words. The hesitation seemed somewhat foolish. They might not even be getting my messages. NASA may not exist anymore for all I knew. A lot of changes can happen in three hundred years. When I left earth, America hadn't even been a country for three hundred years.

Right after entering the space stream, I sent my first message back to earth. I remember it like yesterday. Several firsts happened on that day. First time I talked with Jamie; first time I told Courtney I loved her; the first day a man entered the space stream. Those things made it the best day of my life. Optimism had filled my body like a B-12 shot. Excitement coursed through my veins as I sent off that first message.

This may be my last message. I'm not sure yet.

NASA had no way of getting messages to me. Shortly after entering the space stream, I proved the mathematical impossibility. The space stream was simply moving Chronos too fast away from earth. A message couldn't travel fast enough to catch up to me. I'd never be able to receive earth's messages unless and until I became stationary. Until I landed on Kepler.

Well, I can't find Kepler. How will I ever land there? I'm never going to get my messages.

Over the years, I sent thousands of messages to earth. A few personal ones to Jamie and Courtney, and even a couple to Sarge. They never heard them, of course. Based on my calculations, it took approximately a hundred years for my messages to get back to earth. By the time they arrived, everyone on earth who I loved was already dead, unless scientists had discovered a pill allowing humans to live for a thousand years. I remember hoping they hadn't. I wouldn't recommend anyone live that long.

How would I know? I'm barely going to make it three hundred years.

The day's events looped in my head like a bad B movie.

It started out like any other day. A cup of coffee and breakfast.

Chronos had a large storage area that contained four hundred and fifty different variations of food pills in small packets. More than one million packets were in storage at takeoff, and about twenty-five percent had been used. When a pill was heated, it expanded and became the size of a small portion of food, not unlike a bag of popcorn that expanded when put in a microwave oven. That gave me the experience of eating substance, along with the necessary nutrients.

That morning, my breakfast tasted like eggs, sausage, and pancakes. Three meals and one snack were all I allowed myself to eat each day.

A greenhouse on board facilitated growing fruits and vegetables on a limited basis but I never used it. If Kepler was suitable for growing food, I wanted to save the seeds for when I arrived there.

While the packets of food would last for more than a thousand years, even longer with rationing, practicality and forward thinking helped me plan even beyond a thousand years.

A moot point now. Another regret. I could have been eating whole foods all this time.

After breakfast, I did my usual morning workout.

Weightlessness has a dramatic effect on the human body. To offset those effects, I exercised at least two hours a day. A treadmill on board and a specially designed resistance training machine sufficiently exercised my muscles.

That morning, I did a cardiovascular and a free weight routine. You can't lift free weights in space like you can on earth. Without gravity, hundreds of pounds of weights float and could easily be lifted even by a small child. NASA spent a lot of money creating a device that simulated resistance training. The Advanced Resistance Exercise Device—I called it The Beast—provided all the weight training needed.

More aggressive weight training could be done on that machine, but injury was always a concern to me. I did just enough to make sure I didn't lose strength or body mass without risking injury. Today was not a particularly heavy workout.

After my workout, I took a shower.

Chronos had a big holding tank that held up to a thousand gallons of water. That obviously wasn't enough water to last me a thousand years, so a system was designed to combine hydrogen and oxygen to make water. Called the WOG. Water Oxygen Generator. Once produced, water went through a sophisticated filtering and recycling system providing me with an ample supply of pure drinking water that would last as long as the WOG was working properly.

Every drop of water on the spacecraft was recycled. If I brushed my teeth, which I did that morning, no water was wasted and was returned to the recycling tank. Showers were rare and a luxury. They used too much water. I mostly cleaned myself with sanitized soap and shampoo that came in small packets. When I took a shower, which was about once a month, excess water was captured and sent to the holding tank and filtered. Today happened to be the day of the month for a shower.

The same system that produced the water also produced my oxygen supply. One time, an alarm went off alerting me of a major problem with the WOG. It quit producing oxygen altogether. I had enough oxygen in the compartments to last for a day, and enough stored to last for a week. That could have been a dire situation. Fortunately, it only took me a few hours to fix the problem.

However, that problem made me keenly aware of the risk of a fire. The water and oxygen were produced by a small spark that created combustion which produced the gas that turned into water and oxygen. That spark was not igniting which was why the WOG wasn't working. I fixed it, but my concern was that the spark could combine with the oxygen and start a flash fire. The tools were on board to put out a fire, but a fear of fire was constantly in the back of my mind.

After my shower, I studied.

My first two hundred years were spent studying almost every day, which was the thing I enjoyed doing the most on earth. That really helped to pass the time. While on earth, I earned a bachelor's degree in engineering from Stanford, a MEd, which was a master's in mathematics, from MIT, and a bachelors, masters, and PHD from the University of Pennsylvania in political science just because I could. If I'd had the time, I would have gotten more.

Time was not in short supply on Chronos. By my bicentennial, I'd completed the equivalent of one hundred and seventy-five PHD programs. The computer on Chronos made that possible. Chronos 7 had the most sophisticated computer system available on earth at the time of my departure. Every bit of information known to man was entered into its computer software system. The world, and all its knowledge, was literally at my fingertips.

I developed degree plans complete with tests and curricula. My completed degrees included the fields of science, philosophy, history, political science, computer science, medicine, music theory, and even home economics. Twelve degrees were from Harvard, nineteen from Oxford, six from MIT, and several from other schools. Most were from my school, Adam University.

Dam U for short.

The advantage of owning the school was that I always finished first in my class and always delivered the commencement address.

My one medical degree was from Johns Hopkins. I was a medical doctor in name only, since my developed program was not accredited. In reality, my program was better, harder, and prepared a student more than the actual Johns Hopkins program. Performing an operation was part of the training; although, there was no way for me to get practical experience.

I was fluent in twenty-seven different languages and had fourteen degrees from foreign countries. Those graduation speeches were delivered in their native tongues.

Upon successfully completing the equivalent of two hundred degrees, I quit. Socrates wrote that the only true wisdom was knowing you know nothing. That might be the stupidest thing ever written. No one knows nothing. Everyone knows something. Wisdom was knowing when you knew enough and started applying it. At two hundred degrees, I decided that I knew enough, and started applying what I knew with a vengeance.

Maybe some good has come out of this trip.

Several physics problems had stumped the greatest minds on earth for years. When I solved them, I sent messages with my equations and formulas. I spent a good amount of time on the problems of human suffering.

A complex system for growing food and producing water affordably was perhaps my greatest accomplishment in the first three hundred years. Third world countries could use the technology to end drought and hunger issues.

From an entrepreneurial standpoint, I perfected a means to generate energy and sent back the dimensions of a product that would make electricity unnecessary and obsolete. An application for a patent accompanied the information. The patent wouldn't ever benefit me, but I wanted to own it, nonetheless.

Maybe I should stay alive. I could make more discoveries.

After I studied, I went to view Kepler. That's when my world turned upside down.

Chronos had an observation deck equipped with a high-powered telescope and a sophisticated computer and many astronomy tools. I had been taking readings and measurements of Kepler for several years, trying to learn as much about my final destination as possible.

A few years before, it became apparent that Kepler was changing. The planet was sixty percent larger than earth, yet, as I drew closer, the view of Kepler didn't become clearer; it became cloudier. I studied the phenomenon for months and couldn't come up with an adequate explanation.

I still don't have one.

When the planet started changing dimensions, I was really baffled. The closer we got to Kepler, the smaller it appeared. That, of course, was impossible. Distance and speed are constant in relation to each other. The immutable law of physics applied throughout the universe. Nothing in Physics could explain how an object could become smaller as the distance grew smaller.

Now it's gone altogether. Overnight. Poof... Like a magician's trick.

The observation deck had a lounge area where I could sit and look out at the heavens. I was sitting there thinking about how to explain the new and unbelievable developments that had transpired that day.

I could hear my conversation with NASA in my head.

"Have you checked your telescope? Could there be a malfunction?"

Is it strange that the voice I hear is Sarah's?

"Do you think I'm stupid? That's the first thing I checked. It's working perfectly."

"Did an explosion destroy it?"

"There would be a debris field."

"Did you veer off course?"

"No. The autopilot would've alerted me."

"How are you feeling?"

"I know what you're insinuating with that question."

"I'm not insinuating anything. I'm just asking."

"Am I out of my mind? Have I lost my marbles? Am I off my rocker? Are the lights on and no one is home? Is that what you want to ask?"

"Not in those words."

"Just come out and ask it. 'Am I going insane from spending all these years alone?'"

"Are you?"

"No. I'm perfectly sane. I'm not seeing things. Kepler was there last night, and it's not there today. I don't know why, and I don't care anymore. I have wasted three hundred years of my life on this stupid mission that now I can't finish."

"You can finish the mission."

"How am I supposed to go to Kepler and send back my findings if Kepler doesn't exist?"

I was mad.

"Maybe NASA should have done more research before wasting all this time and money and my life on a worthless mission. I should just end my life and put myself out of all this misery."

"That's ridiculous. Are you going to give up that easily?"

"What's the point? Kepler was the mission. There is no Kepler. There is no mission. This ship is like a prison. I'm willing to do the time if there's a good reason to do so. Now, I'm just ready to get out."

"Let's work the problem, Adam. Kepler can't just disappear without an explanation. Science requires facts. The facts turn into theories. You need to develop a working theory as to what happened to Kepler after you get the facts. Get a hold of yourself. Complete the mission."

"I don't know what happened."

"Aren't you the least bit curious? Do you want to die not knowing?"

That was a good point.

"Don't give up yet. We are counting on you. Quit feeling sorry for yourself. Get to work and get more information and then get back to us."

That's exactly what I'm going to do.

* * *

I got my second wind.

Over three hundred years, I'd gotten my second wind hundreds of times. This time was different. My journal entry for that day summed up my deep introspection.

My whole life had been devoted to the pursuit of knowledge. It's in knowledge that I have always found the truth. I'm now in a search for truth. When I find the truth, I'll find knowledge.

I set down my pencil and contemplated those deep thoughts.

Perhaps that's what Courtney was trying to tell me about God.

Courtney and Jamie made me promise I would read the Bible. When I read a book, I always read the end first, to see if I wanted to finish it. I read the book of Revelation and then quit reading. The Bible was too weird. If the entire Bible was like Revelation, then

I wasn't interested. I finally reconsidered and read through the Bible just to keep the promise, even though my heart wasn't in it.

I should read it again.

I will.

First, what the hell happened to Kepler?

For nineteen hours, I worked on it, nonstop. The more roadblocks, the stronger my resolve. Something monumental was there to be discovered. I could feel it. The truth hovered over me like an eagle hovers over a ledge on a cliff right before it lands. The universe was about to reveal something to me. What was it?

It is my destiny.

My thoughts started rushing in like a flood.

"What if distance and speed are relative just like time is relative?"

"That's not possible."

"Everybody told Einstein time was constant, and he proved them wrong."

"We know that distance and speed are constant. It's been proven."

"People thought the earth was flat, until it wasn't."

"It never was."

"Exactly."

"Just because you perceive distance and speed to be constant, they may be relative based on your perception."

Interesting.

A light bulb went off in my head.

"What if I have already passed Kepler?"

"Again. Not possible."

"Why not? What if in space, distance and speed are relative and measured differently than they are on earth? Time slows down in space. What if velocity accelerates faster in space than on earth?"

"Some laws of physics are constant throughout the universe. Speed's one of them."

"You know from Physics 101 that a person looking at a train from a hundred yards away perceives the speed differently than someone a mile away."

"Perception might be different, but the reality is the same. The train's still traveling at the same speed and will cover the same distance in the same amount of time."

"Not if the train is traveling in space at the speed of light."

"Okay. I see your point."

"It's easy enough to prove one way or the other. All I have to do is look in the telescope. If Kepler is behind me, then at least I'll know a starting point to figure out why."

The telescope was facing forward, so I turned it around and scanned the sky looking for Kepler. At first, I was disappointed that it wasn't there. Then I was encouraged by the fact that it had given me more information. I knew where Kepler wasn't. It wasn't in front of me or behind me. I just didn't know where it was.

What other options are there?

"How can I prove that speed and distance are constant?"

"I can measure the distance between earth and me. It's an easy calculation. If speed and distance are constant, my calculation will be right on the money. If it's not, my calculation will be wrong. If it's wrong, I can calculate how it's different. That'll tell me if speed and distance in space are constant once and for all."

Good idea.

Some quick calculations identified where earth should be in my telescope. While earth was still a long distance away, it would be clearly visible. The entire solar system including all the planets, earth, and the sun should be visible as well.

I blinked my eyes twice as if what I was seeing would somehow magically change. It didn't.

The earth was not there... It had disappeared too.

Chapter Fifteen

That's impossible. Earth can't just vanish into thin air.

"Stop saying that! Just because you don't have the knowledge, doesn't mean it's impossible." Courtney's voice was speaking that thought to me.

I remembered a similar conversation we'd had on earth.

"God doesn't exist," I had said.

"Stop saying that!"Courtney retorted. "Just because you don't believe it, doesn't make it so."

"Just because you believe it doesn't make it so either."

I immediately regretted saying that. Tears welled up in her eyes, and she looked at me with her lips quivering clearly hurt by my words.

"You may not know the truth, but when you do, it will set you free," she said.

I bit my lip so I wouldn't say anything. I didn't want to hurt her again.

"How much knowledge of the entire universe do you possess?" she asked.

"I don't know. Maybe ten percent. Probably not even that much."

"Is it possible that God could exist in the ninety percent of the knowledge you don't possess?" she asked.

That day I changed from being an atheist to an agnostic. Courtney had won that argument. I couldn't say any more with certainty that God didn't exist. The only thing I could say was that I didn't know if he did or not.

"If he does exist, wouldn't you want to know him? Wouldn't you want to discover where he is?" she asked.

The same thing was true with this dilemma. The earth and Kepler had to still exist. I just had to discover where they were.

Yes, Courtney. If God does exist, I would want to know him.

Adam, focus on one mystery of the universe at a time. Don't you have enough to think about already?

I went back to my work and started writing out more formulas. For four hours, I pushed my pencil. The numbers ran together. Nothing made sense.

In physics, when you're trying to prove or disprove a theory, you must keep going back to the beginning and recalculating your formula. If one digit of one line of one equation is wrong, the whole thing will be wrong. You must find what's wrong in the equation in order to get to the right conclusion. Something was wrong in my equation. I had to go back to the basics and rethink my presuppositions.

"Start with what you know. Write it down."

"The universe is flat. Distance and speed are constant..."

What if those are wrong?

A noise interrupted me. A voice... A woman's voice I hadn't heard in three hundred years. Another impossibility.

"Adam, it's me, Courtney."

Maybe I'm going crazy after all.

I listened intently but didn't hear anything more. I went back to work.

Static... Faint, but distinct.

"Chronos 7, Tower. Prepare for a message. Over."

In space, you stay strapped in your chair, so you don't float in the weightlessness. A lap belt held me secure. I loosened it. The observation deck was above the main cabin. The messages were received downstairs. One push off the wall, and I flew down the stairs into the main cabin, almost striking my head on the far wall.

The message was clear. Sarah was speaking.

"Hello Adam. Hope all's well. We just launched another astronaut into the space stream. Her name is Lucy Bedford. Be on the lookout for her. Hopefully, the two of you can find each other. She's headed for Kepler as well."

"Don't send her to Kepler." I wanted to scream at the top of my lungs.

I quickly sent my own message.

"Chronos 7 to Chronos 8, Over. Lucy, this is Adam Lang. I just received a message that you are traveling right behind me. I hope things are going well. Answer me if... when you get this."

The message was sent with optimism. She'd get the message fairly quickly. But hers wouldn't get back to me, because I was moving away from her, but maybe we could somehow find a way to communicate. I had a new dilemma to work on.

How did the messages from earth get to me?

"They can't. It's impossible."

It can't be impossible. I'm getting them.

"What if NASA developed a way to send messages at a faster speed?"

"Even if they did, I'm traveling away from them. They would have to increase the velocity by so much to make up the distance, it would be mathematically impossible. There's no logical way those messages could get from earth to me."

Obviously, that wasn't true. They did get to me, so there had to be a logical explanation.

More messages came. They flooded my inbox. At first, they were from right after the launch. Then they were from years after the launch. They were all arriving at almost the same time. Some messages would arrive ten seconds apart yet were sent ten years apart on earth. The first one hundred years of messages arrived within an hour.

That confused me even more.

"How could a message, sent a hundred years later arrive at the same time as a message sent a hundred years before?"

"Kepler is missing. I'm getting messages from earth. The earth is missing... Lucy is in the space stream. How can I talk to her?"

My head hurt. I let out a loud scream. If aliens were sleeping nearby, I disturbed them. Those thoughts haunted my mind, until I finally fell asleep from the mental exhaustion.

* * *

When I awoke, I couldn't make myself go back to work. I had some alternatives to take my mind off the problem.

Every song ever written was on my computer. My computer also had every episode of every television show ever created up to the time I left earth. Every movie, opera, ballet, play, musical, symphony... they were all on my computer, and over the years, I'd listened and watched as many as I could to pass the time.

"Vegging" out became my pastime, and I noticed that my mind lost some of its sharpness when I did too much of it. It did help to pass the time, and I discovered I enjoyed music more than I ever knew. Television, not so much.

I also had the benefit of artificial intelligence. The computer software program allowed me to create people through virtual reality. I created characters who could interact and carry on conversations with me. Nothing like the real thing, but the voices sounded real, and the avatars were eerily lifelike and better than nothing.

The guys were Ricky, Blake, and Bucky. The girls were Joanne, Christy, and Veronica. A character named Sarge was a scrawny little nerdy guy with glasses who I enjoyed making fun of every chance I got. We got into all kinds of fights, all of which I won. The software program was rigged since I was the one who perfected it. I took some satisfaction in my joke, even if the real Sarge never knew about it.

The characters responded to questions, had facial expressions, and could show emotions. Many hours were spent talking to my "friends." We played games like chess, monopoly, risk, checkers, and scrabble. More than five hundred different games, including various card games, were at our disposal.

On the one hand, they kept me company; on the other hand, they reminded me of what I was missing at home. I considered them a mixed blessing.

A robot was also on board—an extremely lifelike female. She was still in her box in the closet. It seemed too weird to me. I preferred to interact from a distance with my computerized friends. That's how it was for me on earth as well. Looking back, I should've had more friends.

What I wouldn't give to be able to interact with Courtney and Jamie one more time.

I had a new appreciation for the term "killing time." After a few hundred years, I wanted to kill time, slay it, murder it, put it in a coffin, and bury it. Seven hundred more years needed killing. *I won't do it.*

They say that time heals all wounds.

I can say from experience that's not true.

Some wounds never healed, even after many, many, many, years.

* * *

Three hours later, I turned off the music and went back to my work area with new ideas and a new resolve.

It has to do with perspective. Distance and speed are relative based on perspective.

At least I had a starting point. The solution as to why Kepler and earth were missing would be found in the messages. The question was staring up at me from the page.

"How did I receive the messages at the same time even though they were sent at different times?"

Einstein went through this same thing. Think like he thought.

My brain fired off thoughts as fast as a computer.

Einstein proved that just because time appeared to be constant in one scenario didn't mean that was so in every scenario. Hence, time was relative. Events that occurred at the same time for one observer could occur at a different time for another observer.

Time was different in space than on earth, as I had been experiencing for three hundred years. I had two clocks on Chronos. One recorded that I'd been traveling for more than three hundred years. The other said that I'd only been traveling for a little over seven hours.

Relativity. Those on earth perceived the amount of time I traveled differently than I did.

Distance and speed appear to be constant just as time appeared to be constant to Einstein.

"Is it possible for me to experience distance and speed differently in space than how it's observed on earth?"

"The answer has to be no."

"Yet, I'm clearly experiencing the receipt of the messages differently than how the people on earth sent them?"

I rubbed my temples, trying to stimulate something in my brain that would unscramble all this madness. Keep thinking. Processing.

"What about distance? What if they weren't traveling the same distance?"

"They aren't. The messages sent later are traveling a greater distance. That means they should theoretically take even longer to get here."

Back to square one.

"Was it speed that wasn't constant? Was it time that wasn't constant? Was it distance that wasn't constant? Or was it a matter of perspective?"

I considered another possibility.

What if the universe wasn't constant? The universe was expanding but also flat, so the expansion was like a piece of clay expands when it's flattened. Everything in the universe should change proportionately as it expands together.

The speed to travel through it would still be constant.

I considered another possibility.

"What if the universe had hills and valleys in it, and I was in a valley? In Texas, you can see for miles because it's flat. In Colorado, you can only see as far as the mountain in front of you. That could explain why I can't see Kepler or earth."

I thought about that possibility for more than an hour.

"If that were the case, how could you see Kepler from earth? The dip in the universe would block it."

"Not if the earth and Kepler were higher than the highest points where the valleys started. You would still have an unobstructed view."

"Then you would be able to see the dips."

My head hurt again. I went over to my chair and turned the music back on. I set it to play random tunes. I didn't even want to make the decision about what I was going to listen to.

Surprise me.

The first song was a Jim Croce tune. I laughed. *Time in a Bottle.* "That's an oldie." Croce wrote that song more than three hundred and seventy years ago. The irony wasn't lost on me that the song was about time.

"I definitely don't have that problem. I have plenty of time to do the things I want to do."

My mood was improving.

I loved the next song. I Got a Feeling... I started singing along.

I loved black-eyed peas—the food—and I loved Black Eyed Peas, the singing group.

I found myself inspired.

I was tapping my feet. Flailing my arms. Trying to dance. Dancing in space wasn't an easy thing to do. *Thankfully no one can see me.* I wasn't a good dancer anyway. Even worse in space.

The beat was pulsing through my body.

My heart rate was up. My spirits were up. Hope was rushing through my body like a refreshing, ice cold, river.

That song ended. A Spinners song began playing. *Working My Way Back to You.*

Another one of my favorites.

I stood straight up from my chair. So fast that if I hadn't been wearing gravity boots, I would've flown into the ceiling.

That's it! I figured it out. I know where earth is. I know where Kepler is. I know why I am receiving the messages.

Chapter Sixteen

If my theory is true, this will be the greatest scientific discovery of all time.

Like every theory it must be proven by facts, and I set out to find the facts.

My heart was pounding. I was breathless as I rushed into the observation deck to begin my work. Everything had to be documented carefully, and my work area needed to be perfectly organized. A checklist was developed outlining everything needed for my research.

A new journal was started dedicated solely to this new theory. The date and time were noted on the first line. On the next lines, I started a narrative of where I was and what I was doing when I first made the discovery. Careful detail described how the Spinners song triggered the thoughts that led to the discovery. Mainly the line, "I'm making my way back to you."

The steps needed to be recorded for posterity and the formulas and equations written down neatly for all the world to see. The findings would be sent back to earth, of course, but if my theory was correct, I would be returning to earth in just a few years, and my papers and equations would be displayed in a museum, perhaps even a traveling display. Everything had to be preserved and protected.

Fame was not something I sought or desired. Einstein loved the limelight and relished the fame thrust upon him when he discovered the theory of relativity. Mine would be an even greater discovery and would bring me even more renown than Einstein had received.

I couldn't have cared less.

My voyage had kept me in the limelight all these years anyway as the earth received my ongoing messages and I sent back solutions to complicated problems. Several messages from earth stated that I had won several Nobel Prizes for Science and Physics. My formulas had granted me much acclaim in the scientific community.

The idea for developing food and water for third world countries had been implemented and had alleviated ninety percent of all the world's hunger and thirst problems. That message brought me tremendous satisfaction and helped me to realize that the journey and its trials had been worth it.

The Nobel prizes had not been without controversy. Many of my competitors felt I had an unfair advantage since I'd had hundreds of years to work on my formulas and they'd only had a limited life-time. Their arguments were petty and reeked of jealousy. To me, physics and science were not for personal gain but for the advance-ment of knowledge and the improvement of the human race. Who cared how a discovery was made as long as it was? Who cared who made it, as long as somebody did?

Such things were of no concern to me when I was on earth, and even less of a concern in space. I was literally above the fray, mil-lions of miles in outer space away from the self-seeking egomaniacs who were obviously prevalent on earth. That brought me great satis-faction that I could do my work away from all their pettiness.

They could have their fame and I would enjoy my privacy. My ef-forts were not for fame or recognition.

I just wanted to go home.

* * *

The first step was the calculations. They were easy, but I did them carefully, so there would be no mistake. Earth should be in the telescope exactly where my calculations showed it should be. No calculations were done nor necessary as it related to Kepler, so I ignored them altogether.

Step two was visual confirmation.

Armed with my calculations, I went to the telescope, which was already facing the right direction, so no adjustment was necessary. A quick check confirmed that everything was in working order. The search for earth didn't take long. Earth was right where I expected it to be. So were the sun and the other planets of our solar system.

They were in front of me, not behind me.

The first presupposition of my theory was correct. I kept my composure. My next step was to turn the telescope the other direction and began looking behind me. Not for Kepler 452b. It didn't exist. It never did. There was no reason to even try to verify that fact. I was certain of it.

The second part of my theory would explain why astronomers were able to observe Kepler for all these years. It should be easy enough to prove; It just had to be confirmed visually. That took more time and care. I didn't know exactly what I was looking for, but I would know it as soon as I saw it.

Just as I suspected, a slight image of a sliver of a planet not more than a thumbnail size, appeared in my view. It would've been easy to miss if I hadn't been focused on finding it.

Kepler wasn't a planet at all; it was a reflection of a planet.

The next step was to find what was creating the reflection. An unnamed planet just ahead on the left was the culprit. I named the planet Lang 1a. Since I discovered it, I got to name it.

All three arms of my theory were complete. Having all the visual evidence I needed, I created my formula. Two hours later the formula was finished. The mathematics worked out perfectly. My theory was correct.

The universe was not flat after all... The universe was round.

* * *

The day Kepler disappeared was the day I reached the edge of the universe and turned back toward earth in an arc which followed the space stream back in the direction from which I had come. Kepler 452b was merely a reflection of Lang 1a. That was why it appeared cloudy and why its dimensions were decreasing the closer I came to it. Lang 1a was positioned perfectly to reflect light off the back of the universe, creating an image that made it look like a planet.

When I had reached the back of the universe, the image disappeared. I couldn't see Earth behind me, because it was now in front of me. I couldn't see Kepler in either direction because it didn't exist, and I could no longer see the reflection from my angle.

"I'm going back to earth!" I said aloud with utter delight.

It would take me almost three hundred years to get back to earth, but I would eventually get there. Once back on earth, I would begin the aging process again, but it would be well worth it. Even though I would have been gone for six hundred years, I'd have aged by only sixteen hours.

"I wonder if I can collect back pay?"

A smile came on my face as I thought about how much NASA would owe me for six hundred years of salary with annual increases, bonuses, vacation pay, and benefits. I had three hundred years to figure that number out, and I would bring it up when I landed.

The rest of my time in space needed to be used wisely. The possibilities were endless. I could already think of a dozen unsolvable physics problems because they assumed the universe was flat. Now that I knew it was round, I was certain those problems could be solved.

My findings needed to be sent back to earth immediately so the best minds could be working on them as well. Who got the credit was not as important as solving the problems. I'd always get the credit for the foundational discovery, much like how Einstein got the credit for the discoveries that came from his initial work.

Rather than send it back as a message, I created a paper called *The Universe is Like a Balloon*. In it, I explained that the universe was round and expanding, so its dimensions were always changing. A balloon expands when filled with air, its dimensions changing with each breath blown into it. The exact dimensions of the universe as it relates to earth were now available to us. The dimensions on the other end of the balloon were still a mystery, but at least we knew the shape. The earth was likely not the center of the universe, but the other end of the universe could probably be seen from earth when it was on that side of the sun.

Satisfied, I went to bed and slept for hours.

The next day would be another big day.

Something on Lang 1a had piqued my curiosity.

* * *

Four months later

I studied the planet Lang in great detail. Smaller than earth and, unlike earth, Lang didn't rotate on its axis. Therefore, the back side of Lang was away from the sun. From my angle, I could see both sides perfectly. The sunny side was mostly desolate. The backside was out of the view of the earth which was why no one had ever seen it.

The back side showed all signs of being capable of supporting life. Several bodies of water could be easily seen on the surface. The surface also had what appeared to be vegetation growing. If vegetation existed, life existed, and likely oxygen to support life.

The light and darkness on Lang were synchronized as if by design. This created a mystery. No body of light could be producing the light on the back side. The sunny side had light twenty-four hours a day because several sources of light were shining directly on the planet all the time. The back had no such light and should have been in darkness all the time which would have made vegetative growth impossible.

This created a dilemma. One option was to leave the space stream and explore Lang and determine if there was life and find the source of the mysterious light. If it could support life, then I might meet a new life form, which was the reason I took the trip to begin with. If it couldn't support life, I'd be stuck there. It would be impossible to get back into the space stream.

"Half of me wants to do something, but the other half doesn't," was a saying on earth that took on a whole new meaning for me. Half of me was arguing that I should go to Lang; the other half was arguing for Earth.

An argument raged in my head relentlessly.

You should land on Lang.

I want to go home.

Lang is your home. It's even named after you.

I know, I named it.

There might be life on Lang.

There might not be.

That's the whole reason you came on this trip. To discover life on other planets.

If I go down there and get out of the space stream, I'll never get back into it.

You have plenty of food and water to last for years.

I want to go home.

It'll take three hundred years to get back to earth. You can get out of this spacecraft in a few short months.

I like the sound of that.

This is your chance to live in infamy. You discovered the universe is round, now you can discover life on other planets. You are the modern-day Christopher Columbus.

The entry is too dangerous. I don't have enough time to prepare.

You can figure it out. If you can't figure it out, you can always abort.

They might not be friendly. They could shoot me out of the sky as soon as I enter their air space.

You might find a wife there. Have some little aliens. Doesn't that sound like fun?

You're sick.

They might think you are like the Wizard of Oz and make you the king of the world.

Let's get serious. Suppose I decide to go to Lang. First, I have to survive entry. That's no sure thing. I have no idea what the atmosphere is like, and I might burn up as soon as I enter it. That's assuming I get the calculations right. If I'm off even a few degrees, I'll hit the atmosphere and skip off into space. If I come in too steep, I'll burn to a crisp. You know how much I am afraid of fire.

That last thought caused me to shudder.

"I'll be out of the space stream, tumbling around to God knows where. If I survive all that, I'm going to land on a planet that might or might not have oxygen. If it does, I might venture out of the spacecraft and catch some organism or bacteria that causes a disease that might mean a long and horrible death. Even if it doesn't, I'll start aging immediately and will die in a few years anyway."

He shrugged his shoulders. "At least you'll know. Life is a risk. You took a risk even coming on this mission. This is your destiny. This is your calling. Your finest hour. The entire world is watching. You're the man of the hour. It's up to you."

"I want to go home."

Then the messages from earth took an alarming turn, and the decision was made for me.

* * *

The first messages were concerning, but not alarming. All of them arrived within one hour, meaning the events depicted in the messages all happened within a hundred-year period of time on earth.

With each message, the circumstances on earth became more dire.

The earth was seeing a significant increase in earthquakes, hurricanes, tornadoes, typhoons, tsunamis, fires, and famines. The United States was having a major earthquake just about every day. A large quake struck California and had created an entirely new coastline. Millions died. An earthquake in the central part of the country doubled the width of the Mississippi River, devastating the cities along its bank and destroying New Orleans, leaving it completely underwater. Tens of thousands were dead in the heartland of America.

The messages began to describe unrest throughout the world. Wars and rumors of wars were happening on every continent. Troops were amassing for a major conflict in the middle east. Russia, China, and the Muslim countries had surrounded Israel. The United States and her allies were the only barrier preventing its annihilation.

One particular message marked the beginning of the end.

"Adam, more than a billion people are missing off the face of the earth. No one knows what happened to them or where they went. There's talk they were abducted by aliens. It's utter chaos everywhere."

Then the messages became chilling.

"Adam, it's horrible. You wouldn't even recognize Earth. There's a man who thinks he's the ruler over the entire world. He's trying to create calm and restore order, but it's not working. The United States is refusing to recognize him as the world leader. War is inevitable. He's imprisoning and killing everyone who doesn't follow him. We're probably going to war."

More chaos... Panic.

"Adam, all hell has broken loose in the middle east. They're fighting right now in a place called Armageddon. This may be the end of the world as we know it. We don't know how long we'll be able to keep broadcasting. We've sent dozens of messages to Lucy, but we've never heard back from her. We don't know if she's alive or dead.

Maybe you know. Hopefully, the two of you can communicate and meet somewhere."

And then the messages stopped altogether.

My hopes of returning to earth were dashed. In some ways, I was relieved. The thought of another three hundred years in the space-craft wasn't something I was looking forward to. At the same time, I grieved for my planet. I didn't know anyone there, but I was a part of them, and they were a part of me.

I remembered reading Revelation in Courtney's Bible. Some of our conversations even dealt with what she called the "end times."

I went down to my computer and pulled up everything I could find about what the Bible said would happen in the last days. Several passages described what I'd just heard in the messages. I wrote down Matthew 24, 1 John 2:18, and Revelation 16:16. The Bible was still by my bedside. I found the passages and began reading in Matthew 24. When I read verses six and seven, I stopped and read it out loud.

"And you will hear of wars and threats of wars, but don't panic. Yes, these things must take place, but the end won't follow immediately. Nation will go to war against nation, and kingdom against kingdom. There will be famines and earthquakes in many parts of the world."

The message said there were major earthquakes. California. Millions, dead. The messages talked of wars. Jesus said there would be many wars.

"How did Jesus know what was going to happen centuries later?"

Missing people. No explanation. The rapture? Courtney had talked about it. Jesus mentioned it as well. He read through the rest of the chapter until he came to verses thirty-nine through forty-one.

"That's the way it will be when the Son of Man comes. Two men will be working together in the field; one will be taken, the other left. Two women will be grinding flour at the mill; one will be taken, the other left."

An eerie feeling came over me. Jesus knew what was going to happen centuries before it did. He was predicting it like a prophet.

There'd be a ruler... Tyrant. He'd take over the world. The Antichrist.

First John 2:18 spoke of him.

"Dear children, the last hour is here. You have heard that the Antichrist is coming, and already many such antichrists have appeared."

Several other places in the Bible talked about a man who would come and take over the world and rule with an iron fist.

Armageddon. A final battle. The end of the world. My jaw dropped as I read Revelation 16:16. Right there in the Bible. Plain as day.

"Then they gathered the kings together to the place that in Hebrew is called Armageddon."

Written thousands of years before...

How did the Bible predict the end of the world would happen at Armageddon?

A loud bang... Followed by an explosion. An alarm sounded—more of a siren. It grew louder. Deafening. Smoke.

A fire alarm.

Chapter Seventeen

T he shattering high-pitched shrill of the fire alarm resounded throughout Chronos like a bell in a watch tower.

Why does it have to be so loud?

I was terrified as I rushed down to the lower compartment.

My worst fears were confirmed as smoke rolled out from under the door from the room that housed the oxygen machine.

I let out a weak scream which only managed to cause me to breathe in my first plume of smoke. My lungs burned as I inhaled and tasted the chemicals of the oxygen compound mixing with the smoke.

This is not good.

The protocol called for me to ignore the fire and not even try to put it out until I was safely in my fire suit. The suit was specially designed by NASA to protect me from fire, burns, and chemical burns. The mask covered my entire head and was attached to a small oxygen tank that allowed me to breathe freely while I fought the fire.

The suit and mask were a giant pain. Putting them on was cumbersome and time consuming and limited my range of mobility, making it harder to fight the fire. I had complained about it every time we had a fire drill, but it had fallen on deaf ears.

I made a critical mistake.

Instead of going for the room that held my fire suit, I went directly to the source of the fire to assess the seriousness of it. If I could put out the fire without having to get into the suit, then I would save myself a lot of trouble. If I took the time to get into the suit, the fire could get worse. If the fire was worse than it appeared, and I couldn't put it out quickly, I'd go back and get in the suit.

When I opened the door to the room, I was instantly hit with a plume of black, toxic smoke mixed with more chemicals. I gasped for a breath, inhaling more of the chemicals and sending a burning sensation through my throat, chest, and lungs. My eyes stung as the chemicals released from the fire singed my face and temporarily blurred my vision.

The mask would have protected me from that.

Too late now.

There appeared to be more smoke than fire, so I rushed to get the fire extinguisher. Ignoring the suit and mask sitting next to it, I grabbed the extinguisher and headed back to the fire. As I tried to release the safety seal on the tab, it broke off, rendering it useless. I threw it against the wall and went to get water to pour on the fire.

The water only made the smoke worse and harder for me to breathe. Smoke inhalation became a concern. I was desperately trying to catch my breath as less air and more smoke filled my lungs. The more I breathed in, the more the chemicals burned my throat and lungs. I had to choose between holding my breath or breathing in painful and damaging toxins.

I should have at least put my mask on.

A serious breach in protocol. No matter how serious the fire was, an astronaut was trained to protect himself from the fire first. I was quickly learning why.

An explosion became an immediate concern. The machine was still manufacturing oxygen which was feeding the fire. A small stream was coming out of the pipe, but enough to keep the fire going. No time to don the mask at that point.

One final option was still available to put out the fire. A different extinguisher, considered a last resort, released a chemical spray that would put out the fire on contact. Care had to be taken using it because if it got on any part of my body, it would burn me like acid. I went back to the compartment that housed the fire-fighting equipment, grabbed the container, and rushed back to the fire.

This time, the safety valve released properly as I inched closer to the fire. The problem with this extinguisher was that you had to be right next to the fire before you could release the flame-retardant chemicals. If I released them too soon, they'd float off in the air, and I'd risk breathing them in and getting them on my skin. I needed to be within three feet of the fire.

Sparks being fed by oxygen were flying out of the machine as I cautiously approached. It looked like a sparkler on the fourth of July. They danced and moved almost in unison. The switch to turn off the oxygen was on the side of the box. I considered turning it off, but I couldn't reach it without seriously burning my left arm. That would be my last resort.

I edged closer to the fire and when I got as close as humanly possible, I released the spray.

The machine exploded.

The spray from the extinguisher blew back into my face along with shards of hot metal that seared my face and arm.

The left side of my body took the bulk of the blast. The hair on my arm, leg, and chest were singed off. The skin literally peeled from the bone on my left arm. It rendered my arm useless, and I could feel my arm dangling at my side, unresponsive to any commands.

The blast sent me tumbling across the room. I was temporarily stunned by the concussion of the force as I desperately struggled to get my bearings. The room turned suddenly dark where there had been light moments before.

The darkness wasn't from the loss of light in the cabin.

I was blind.

How come I don't feel any pain?

I remembered that most fire victims don't feel pain at first. The fire burns the nerve endings that carry pain to the brain. Pain would confirm the burns weren't that bad.

Pain would confirm that I'm still alive.

Suddenly... pain. On my face.

I reached for my face with my good right hand but had the awareness to stop myself. Chemicals on my hands would do more damage had I rubbed my eyes or tried to rub my face.

Then excruciating pain.

As if someone had thrown acid in my face. In essence, they had.

At least I'm alive. That's the only consolation. Maybe...

Disbelief.

The smell of burning flesh.

I had partial sight in my right eye. Vision enough to float back over to the room where the fire had started. Thankfully, the explosion had put the fire out. It destroyed the machine and cut off the flow of oxygen to it. With no oxygen feeding the fire, it extinguished itself.

How will I fix it?

That's the least of my worries.

It would take several minutes for the ventilation system to clear the spacecraft of the smoke so I could assess the damage. At least the fire was out. Smoke doesn't rise in a weightless environment, so I instinctively floated to the ceiling to protect myself from further inhalation.

When the smoke cleared, I had the presence of mind to float across the room and attach a tether around my right wrist so I wouldn't float around and bump into the walls.

At that moment, I just wanted to die.

"God, help me!" I cried out. "Please help me."

Mercifully, I passed out.

* * *

I had no idea how long I was unconscious. I awakened with many thoughts.

What was I going to do now?

I should have put on the suit.

"Too late for that now. What's done is done. Remember rule number one in a crisis."

Don't make a bad situation worse. *I made things much worse by not putting on the suit.*

Don't make them worse now.

Think. Assess. Ignore the pain.

I had a high tolerance for pain, but this was pushing my limits. I was completely blind in my left eye, but there was partial sight in my right. I didn't need to look in a mirror to know that the left side of my body was severely burned. Messages to my left arm and hand begging them to move, were met with no response. My left leg and foot did respond telling me that the burns were mostly from the waist up. The right side of my body was largely uninjured.

I untethered my wrist and floated over to assess the oxygen machine.

Completely destroyed. Beyond repair.

I remembered my training. *In a bad situation, be thankful for anything positive. Draw strength from it. Things could always be worse. Don't make it so.*

My mind was racing. How could things be any worse?

You could be dead.

That wouldn't be worse. That would be better.

Maybe the machine can be fixed.

I can't fix the machine with one arm and one eye. I don't think it could be fixed with two good arms and two good eyes.

You still have seven days of oxygen in the reserve tanks.

Then what.

You can land on your planet in three days.

I can't land with one arm.

Worry about that later. You need to treat your wounds.

Chronos had a medical area which had rarely been used. It had various drugs for any type of ailment. If it didn't have the drug, it had the chemicals, and I could formulate the drugs. It also had a robotic surgical arm that could perform any surgery on my body.

I floated over to the area and stopped in front of a mirror to assess the injuries. None of the injuries appeared to be immediately life-threatening.

"That's too bad. I would be better off if the explosion had killed me," I muttered under my breath.

There's nothing I can do for my left eye, though. I don't think the sight can be restored.

The left side of my face had sustained third degree burns. If I were walking down the street, my best friend wouldn't recognize me. "I look hideous."

"You didn't look that good before."

I managed a slight grin.

What about your arm?

My left arm had suffered fourth degree burns. My left leg was burned but would heal in time. I pulled out a strong antibiotic and considered taking a strong pain pill as well. I read the warning label. "May cause drowsiness, and don't operate any heavy machinery. Chronos would be considered heavy machinery."

A milder pain pill allowed me to keep my faculties to better deal with this situation. If I couldn't resolve them, I would take the medication and wait to die. Pills were in the medicine kit that would make dying seem pleasant.

My throat burned as the pills navigated their way through the raw, barren, and charred wilderness that was now my throat. The cool water stung at first but brought soothing relief as it washed away the chemicals I could still taste in my mouth.

A wet towel cleaned the chemicals off my right hand, and I dabbed the right side of my face to remove any other chemicals and to bring relief to it. I didn't dare touch my left side. The towel could pull off any remaining flesh still hanging on.

Drops in my right eye didn't improve my sight but stopped the burning. I spread a salve over my left side and on my face. It didn't bring any noticeable relief because I couldn't feel those areas, but it would help with the healing.

Why didn't you put any on your left arm?

There's no use. I don't want to waste it.

Why would it be wasted?

Because my arm has to be amputated.

* * *

I was in deep trouble.

The oxygen supply would run out in seven days. I could barely see. My left arm was useless. The left side of my body had limited mobility. Landing on Lang was an option, but I would probably burn up in the entry. If I didn't, the ship would still have to land. If I somehow managed to survive the landing, if there was no oxygen on the planet, I'd have the same problem I had now; I'd run out of oxygen in seven days.

Other than that, I can't complain.

"What are your odds? Five percent if I try to land on Lang. Zero percent if I stay here."

I remembered what Jim Lovell said about his problems on Apollo 13. Giving up wasn't an option he ever considered.

"I've considered it."

"What are you going to do?"

"I'm going to my planet."

Five percent is better than zero percent.

* * *

The biggest issue was the entry. My calculations had to be within two degrees to survive the entry. Many unknowns made accuracy impossible. One unknown was how the spacecraft would react to leaving the space stream after all these years. The simulator tried to duplicate it, but this would be the real thing and no simulator could replicate the speed, so it couldn't replicate the outcome.

The exact moment to leave the stream had to be precise. Chronos would go from traveling at 200,000 miles per second, to approximately 17,500 miles per hour. Such a huge difference in velocity made the margin of error miniscule. If I left too soon or too late, I would miss Lang altogether. The math formula was so complicated I didn't feel up to tackling it. Fortunately, the computer made that calculation. I just had to trust it.

If I somehow hit the right entry point, I had no data about Lang's atmosphere and no time to develop it. Things such as gravitational pull and composition were all factors that had to be considered. Exact figures had to be entered into the computer so that the autopilot could fly the spacecraft. It took years to perfect the calculations on earth. I had two days. Deceleration and drag were tricky calculations and would determine how smooth the entry would be. If the calculations were off, the spacecraft could break apart if descending at the wrong speed or pitch.

For a while, the troubling calculations took my mind off my injuries—momentarily.

I contemplated the much-needed amputation. What would be the point? I probably won't survive entry, so why put myself through that if I don't have to?

"I could do it when I land, but only if there's oxygen on Lang."

Again, what's the point? I only had a few days of oxygen left in reserve.

If I survive the landing, and there's no oxygen on Lang, it's going to be a short stay. If I do survive, and there is oxygen, I'll cut it off the day after I land.

You'll survive. You have to. You're the last best hope for mankind.

That's true. I may be the only person left alive in the entire universe.

What about Lucy?

No one has heard from her. I sent her a message telling her where I was landing.

If she's alive, maybe she'll find you and the two of you can hook up and repopulate the universe.

"Shut up!" I said to myself emphatically. Finally putting a stop to the ridiculous train of thought in my head.

If I'm the last best hope for mankind, mankind is in trouble.

* * *

For two days, I'd been admiring my future home, or what might be my final resting place. Lang was a beautiful planet up close. It looked similar to earth from my vantage point. Large bodies of water were evident through the telescope. There also appeared to be beautiful green foliage. It became more and more likely that life was on Lang. Maybe not life as I knew it but at least the possibility to sustain life.

The anticipation had buoyed my spirits. Until I thought about the entry.

Entry into a planet's atmosphere from space was the most dramatic thing an astronaut did. At least ten things had to go right to be successful, and only one of those ten had to go wrong for disaster to strike.

My calculations for trajectory, pull, deceleration, drag, friction, gravity, and resistance all had to be accurate. The heat shield had to sustain the heat of entry which could get as high as fifteen hundred degrees. The spacecraft had to handle the shock of the G forces. Friction from the atmosphere and deceleration could cause up to 3gs of force against the spacecraft.

I would feel it as well. Differently than the intensity astronauts feel when leaving the atmosphere. Primarily because of the rapid deceleration. My chair would be positioned so that I was facing the direction of acceleration, limiting the forces against my body. Even then, astronauts often temporarily blacked out as they had less blood flowing to the brain. The increased pressure on the retinal arteries could also cause temporary blindness. I was already blind in one eye and impaired in the other, so I would probably not notice that. The hope was that the entry did not permanently damage my good eye.

I gingerly made my way to my seat and painfully strapped myself in, every movement was tedious labored. A layer of clothes under my spacesuit protected my wounds from the straps as they would press against my body from the forces of entry. Pain was inevitable. Several pain pills I'd taken a few hours before had barely made a dent.

I said a quick prayer. Over the past two days, I'd found myself praying to God for the first time in my entire life. It might not help, but it couldn't hurt. In some ways, I could feel a presence. Maybe God... maybe Courtney. Maybe both.

* * *

When the time came, Chronos left the space stream with a jolt. The spacecraft began to roll, but the autopilot quickly corrected. The deceleration created sensations of something pushing against my body. Chronos creaked and moaned as the forces of deceleration tested the limits of its structure. It held together, but I couldn't help thinking that any more pressure and Chronos would have torn apart.

I hope there's no damage to the heat shield.

It would take about twelve minutes to enter Lang's atmosphere after leaving the space stream. For a moment, I wondered if the severe jolt had thrown Chronos off its course. If it did, the autopilot had time to correct its course if working properly. If it didn't have time, I would know soon enough. Nothing I could do about it now, strapped in my seat.

No turning back by that point. Fate had taken over. There'd been several times on the journey when I'd cheated death. Live or die, my journey was coming to an end. I would never go back into space again. Reentering the space stream wasn't possible even if I wanted to. I didn't want to. My decision was made and I had no regrets.

I could manage my injuries. The robotic surgical unit would remove my arm. That should stop the risk of infection. The other injuries would heal. My face would be permanently scarred, but if no one was around to see it but me, then I could manage.

"I hope I don't scare the natives."

Hide the women and children.

The twelve minutes flew by. I chuckled at my pun. The moment of truth had arrived.

I braced for entry. With my right hand, I gripped the handle literally as if I was holding on for dear life. Maybe I was. My left arm hung limply by my side, unable to even grip the handle. My wrist was strapped to the chair so it wouldn't flail around during entry.

I tensed my entire body for a shock that never came. The entry was so smooth it seemed like it hadn't actually happened.

I looked out the window half expecting to see Chronos bouncing off into deep space.

Instead, the most breathtaking sight filled my window. Nothing like what I'd ever seen in my life.

Colors.

The most vibrant colors imaginable. All the colors of the rainbow converged into a kaleidoscope of beauty. As a kid, I remembered looking at the beautiful patterns and images in a kaleidoscope. Nothing compared to the rich, vibrant patterns I saw through my window.

Rainbows. Pastels. Bright, bright colors. Blinding if I wasn't already.

I strained to see more.

What's that?

"Are those birds?"

Excitement welled up inside of me.

If there are birds, there's oxygen.

Was there oxygen on Lang?

"I might as well find out."

I'd turned off the oxygen in the spacecraft to reserve what was left in my tank and was relying on the oxygen tank in my spacesuit. Once under ten thousand feet, if there was oxygen on the planet, it would fill my spacecraft and I could breathe without my suit.

I took off my helmet—a complicated process with one hand, but I managed to slide it off.

I can breathe! Beautiful, deep, filling, breaths.

Lang had oxygen. It felt good on my burned lungs. Breathing real oxygen for the first time in three hundred years sent bursts of adrenaline through my veins. My other senses were alive.

I could smell the planet. Fragrances. Aromas.

I could almost hear the sounds of birds singing and radiating in my ears, even though I knew it was impossible to hear them.

The landing. I must stick the landing.

My last obstacle to surviving.

Hope turned to fear. I wanted to explore the new planet. What a shame it would have been to die in the landing without ever getting the chance to explore it.

I purposely programmed the computer to fly a few miles before it set down on the surface. I didn't want a rough landing. The spot I picked was between two ridges.

I hope I made the right choice.

It was.

The landing was smooth as silk. Chronos glided gently to a halt.

"I survived! I'm on the ground."

A feeling came over me unlike any other I'd ever experienced. I pumped my right fist in the air. A huge yell burst out of me like a geyser exploding out of the earth.

I began to cry. Tears of joy.

Two days before, I was without hope; today hope abounded.

I paused for a moment and looked up to God and said, "Thank you."

Chapter Eighteen

I f intelligent life existed on Lang, I assumed they would come quickly. I made a beeline for the observation deck just in case. If they were coming, I wanted advance warning.

Beeline was hardly the right word. Going from total weightlessness to gravity, meant that I had to learn how to walk all over again. My joints and muscles screamed in protest as gravity gripped my body like a vise, forcing every part of me downward. When I first stood from my seat and tried to walk, I staggered around the spacecraft like a drunk leaving a bar.

Even talking was a chore as my lips, tongue, and mouth had to come together differently in gravity to form words. For the first ten minutes, I sounded like a baby babbling. It would be better if no aliens showed up on my doorstep. They would find a hideously deformed, babbling drunk. Their first impression of a man from earth wouldn't be a good one.

From my vantage point in the observation tower, I could have been looking out at western Kansas. Chronos landed in the middle of what looked like a dried river basin surrounded by craggy mountains and dotted with green foliage. It gave the appearance of being desert like, but the outside temperature read a perfect seventy-two degrees. A mysterious glow, which couldn't be explained but I was anxious to explore, hovered in the sky over the mountain to the east.

My landing area showed no signs of the vibrant colors I'd seen in entry. Perhaps they were over the hill and were causing the glow.

I was tempted to leave the spacecraft and hide in the mountains nearby. My physical condition made that option impossible. So, I sat in the tower waiting on high alert for whatever form or shape might appear coming over the hills.

Chronos was equipped with an arsenal of weapons, including some serious firepower, but starting a "war of the worlds" was not my intent. Even if I could win a firefight, I didn't travel millions of miles to kill something. Diplomacy was my best option. If the aliens had weapons, I would talk myself out of the situation, even though I wouldn't know their language. I'd figure something out if the time came.

After several hours, no one came.

Looking out into nothingness got boring after a while.

They don't seem anxious to meet me.

Probably a good thing for them. I look like a freak in a carnival show.

The burns had formed huge blisters on my face. My left eye was swollen shut with puss leaking from it. My eyebrows were completely singed off. My left arm looked like it was bandaged by a first grader. I hadn't showered or shaved since the accident, and my hair was mussed from my spacesuit. Death warmed over, looked better than I did.

My spirits were good even if I didn't look like they were. My feet were on the ground and the possibility of discovering life on another planet was exhilarating.

If they were coming, I began to wonder what they would look like.

Hollywood's depictions of aliens had always amused me. I had my own idea what they looked like, but what I'd seen in movies or television wasn't it. They looked somewhat like humans in my mind. If God was behind the creation of the universe, I was sure that if he created life on other planets, they'd all look similar. Somewhat like me, or at least what I used to look like.

Not little green men.

I wonder if their girls are pretty.

If they are, they might be mad at us for not including them in the Miss Universe pageant.

That thought made me laugh out loud.

"I do miss the companionship of the female persuasion," I mumbled to myself.

Why do I talk like that? How am I ever going to get a date with a hot alien using words like that?

I'm not going to get a date looking like this anyway.

Three hundred years is a long time to be without a woman's touch.

I'm not sure I'm ready to be touched by an alien.

What would I even say?

I've never been good with pickup lines.

Try to think of some.

How about, "Are you an alien, 'cause you abducted my heart?"

I groaned.

What's your sign?

No. That didn't work on earth, I doubt it would work here.

Ugh...

If I told you that you had a celestial body, would you hold it against me?

I'm pathetic.

Would you like to have a close encounter of the Earth kind?

That's enough. *They're going from bad to worse.*

A couple hours of watching and waiting made me less optimistic there was even life on the planet. I presumed if there was, they would've already tried to contact me. My hopes were being dashed with each passing moment. After three hundred years alone, I was starving for companionship. The thought of more years alone on this planet with no other intelligent life, wasn't something I looked forward to.

To get my mind off that possibility, my attention turned to looking for water. No bodies of water were within my immediate sight. There had to be water nearby because there was green foliage. I'd hoped to land close to water so I wouldn't have to carry it for miles with one arm.

One arm... I guess now was as good a time as any to think about that.

When should I do it?

"Tomorrow. In the morning for sure," I said hesitantly.

Maybe the aliens have a hospital. They might have a doctor who can save the arm.

Can't wait any longer. It's already infected. Another day, and I might as well not bother. If the infection gets in my bloodstream, I'm a goner.

I should be asleep for the operation.

No way. I don't trust the robot. I want to be awake in case it makes a mistake.

The procedure called for me to be put to sleep and awakened a couple of hours after surgery. Being asleep was not an option. If something went wrong, I could literally die on the operating table. If I were awake through the procedure, then I could respond to any emergency and try and fix it myself if the robot couldn't.

NASA discouraged that and implored us to trust the robot. They prepared for the possibility that it might be mentally challenging. They understood how difficult it would be to place your life in the hands of a robot. We did it on earth. Most surgeries were performed by robotic arms, but a human was still monitoring the robot.

The robot was more skilled than a human. The risk of the robot malfunctioning or doing something wrong was always there, but it was not as great as the chance for human error when you placed your life in the hands of a doctor.

Tomorrow, I'll just have to hope and pray that everything turns out okay.

To get my mind off the operation, I tried to think of other things. The mystery of the light still confounded me. A search of the sky with the telescope upon landing confirmed that no sun was in the sky, and no logical explanation was found for the light.

Even more confusing was when the sky illuminated into a beautiful sunset signaling darkness was nearing. I described it as a sunset even though no sun was shining on the planet. The sky was painted with glistening bright colors, creating a mural of brilliant shades of pinks, reds, gold, and blue bouncing off each other like a laser light display.

How could there be light and darkness and a sunset, if there's no sun?

Now was not the time to figure it out. That would be for another day. I was tired and ready to go to bed. Tomorrow was going to be an eventful day. It felt strange getting into my sleeping bag without strapping myself in. I barely remembered what it was like to sleep on earth with gravity.

The best night's sleep I'd had in years.

* * *

I readied the robot for the operation. I was having second thoughts.

Am I sure I know what I'm doing?"

I'm sure. I'm a doctor.

You're not even a real doctor.

Close enough.

I think I should get a second opinion. I laughed out loud.

I kept cracking myself up. I guess it was helping me relieve the tension.

I verbally went through my checklist.

"Did you check all the computer instructions for the robot?"

"Checked and double checked. They're correct."

"The blade is sharpened."

"I don't want any jagged edges. It needs to be a clean cut."

"That gave me the creeps. It looked like an executioner sharpening his blade before he chopped his victim's head off."

"Time to put the IV in my leg so hold still."

A saline solution would make sure I was hydrated during the surgery.

"I really should put a sedative in the IV. Help me to relax."

"No. I want to have my full faculties."

I already don't have my full faculties. This is crazy.

Bleeding was the primary risk of the surgery. The tourniquet had to be applied to the upper arm at just the right pressure. If too tight, it could damage the upper arm. Too loose and I would bleed out.

My left arm was lying awkwardly on the table. Strapped in three places, with no mobility. If I'd been asleep, I could just lay there. Wanting to watch everything, I had to sit up and twist my body in a contortion in order to watch the surgery in the monitor with my good eye.

"I think that's everything. Are you ready, Adam?"

No! I'm not ready, but here goes.

I pushed the button and the robot roared to life. It went straight to work preparing for the surgery. The tourniquet tightened. Blade spinning.

What was that?

I thought I'd heard a knocking sound coming from the main cabin.

I shut the robot down for a moment and listened carefully. Not hearing anything, I turned it back on.

Then I heard it again. Definitely a knocking noise.

I instinctively called out, "Is anyone there?"

There it is again.

I needed to unhook the IV and release my arm from the tourniquet. Once free, I went to the window to see who or what was there.

The window on the door would allow me to see outside. No one from the outside could see in, but I wasn't taking any chances as I cautiously peeked through the window. Nothing was visible through the window.

The observation deck gave me a 360-degree view. I looked in every direction, but again nothing was there. If the alien was hiding close to the craft or standing next to it, I wouldn't be able to see him from that vantage point.

The knock was real. I wasn't imagining it. The possibilities were pulsating through my mind like a wave machine in an amusement park. Perhaps the alien knocked but left because no one answered. I dismissed that possibility. I would've seen him from the observation deck if he walked away. If the alien was in some type of flying craft, then I would've heard him leaving. He was still there. I could feel him.

Another, much louder knock startled me. I rushed to the storage area to get a weapon. A complete cache of weaponry was at my disposal. Semi-automatic and automatic rifles were neatly organized in the armory. Handguns, pistols, knives, and grenades were at my disposal. I even had laser weapons on board that could kill a person, or life form as the case might be, instantly.

Heavier artillery was on board to fight off a small army, but I didn't think that would be necessary. More than one alien, if it had been an army... I would've seen them. I opted for something smaller. A Glock G139, a palm-sized gun easy to shoot and even easier to conceal. I chambered a round which was not easy to do with one hand.

The process of opening the door took several steps. The procedures were more complex than just pushing a button. A series of numbers had to be entered. NASA didn't want it to open easily. They didn't want an astronaut inadvertently hitting the wrong button and opening the door and being sucked out into space. I was surprised I still remembered the numbers without having to look them up after all these years.

The door opened from the middle. The top half slid into an above compartment, and the lower half opened outward creating a ramp. As the door opened, I could make out the form of a figure. I wasn't accustomed to the outside light, and it took a moment for my good eye to focus.

A man was looking directly at me.

"Hello, Adam," he said. "My name is Elias."

How did he know my name?

Chapter Nineteen

T he alien who stood outside my spacecraft was the same as me, only different.

The same in the sense that he was remarkably human. Two arms, two legs, two hands, ten fingers, and facial features identical to man. Different in that he was completely naked.

Even though he wore no clothes, his body was surrounded by an aura, a glow that radiated out like a force field, covering anything that would be considered private on earth. It created a sense of modesty for my benefit, although he seemed completely unashamed. The glow was as much a part of him as if he were wearing clothes.

Elias had dark wavy shoulder length hair, carefully parted in the middle, bushy eyebrows, a full beard, and perfect features. The thought occurred to me that he looked like the pictures of Jesus I had seen back on earth.

He headed up the ramp toward me.

"Stop!" I shouted. "Don't come any closer."

He ignored my commands and kept walking until he was inside the threshold of the spacecraft.

I backed up several steps and raised the gun from my side.

"I'm not afraid to shoot."

He looked at the gun with a puzzled look. It occurred to me that he'd probably never seen a gun before and had no idea it could kill him. He clearly had no weapon on him and didn't seem the least bit threatening. But I wasn't willing to take any chances.

He took two more steps forward and said, "Adam, I have a message for you."

"How do you know my name?"

"God told me your name," he said with authority.

The stranger was speaking in his own language, a strange and unknown tongue, yet I was hearing his words in English. He obviously understood what I was saying as well.

How does he know God?

Without realizing it, I had lowered the gun. A deep breath, let out as a sigh, made me realize I suddenly wasn't feeling as strong. Out of the corner of my eye, I could see the IV bag hanging from the operating table, reminding me of my wounds, my weaknesses that were no match for any confrontation if one was to come.

The gentle tone of his voice told me I could trust him, and no confrontation was imminent. He said God had told him my name, and I wanted to believe him. How else could he have known it?

He intercepted my messages to Lucy. Did I mention my name in the messages? I must have. It's a trick.

I bit my lip, holding back the accusations.

I raised the gun again with new resolve. As he took another step toward me out of the light of the doorway, I got a better look at him. He was tall, muscular, but not overly so. A natural leanness not sculpted in a gym. No evidence of pretense or guile. No showiness or attempt to intimidate me with his manner. Fair skin, thick lips. A faint smile.

I returned my focus to his words, trying to process and understand what he was saying.

"When did God tell you my name?" I asked skeptically.

"An angel of the Lord came to me in a dream."

He said it so sincerely.

"The angel called out my name, Elias." He paused. His words were careful, confident, convincing. He continued. "I said to the angel, 'Yes, Lord. I'm here.'"

Elias looked around the spacecraft for the first time, taking in his surroundings, probably curious. *Maybe scouting his enemy, looking for anything worth stealing.* He didn't seem like an enemy or a thief, but he was blocking my exit. *Was that on purpose?*

My finger was still on the trigger of the gun, but I couldn't imagine pulling it. The story was deeply fascinating, and I was riveted by the details. Skeptical but intrigued. Wanting to see how it ended.

"What did the angel say next?" I asked impatiently, wanting him to get to the gist of the dream.

"Go over to the valley of Ashram," he continued at his own pace. "There's an object there that you've never seen before."

My spacecraft?

The story was becoming stranger by the minute. If he was making it up, he was very imaginative.

"There's a man there named Adam. Don't be afraid of him. Tell him God has sent you."

God sent you to me?

The story suddenly took an unbelievable turn. He was losing his credibility.

Why would the God of the universe be the least bit concerned about me? I've never given him a second thought.

Yet, I wanted to believe him. Every fiber of my being wanted this creature, this man, this alien, to be telling me the truth. I'd discovered life on another planet. My mission was accomplished. He was nothing like what I had imagined, nothing like what I had trained for. Was he too good to be true? No way to find out except to keep asking questions, keep probing, keep searching for the truth.

"How do I know that you're telling me the truth?" I asked. Half as a question and half as an admission that I already believed him.

"God said to lay hands on you, and that you would receive back your sight and be healed of your wounds. Your healing would be a sign."

Excitement pulsed through my veins. *Could this possibly be true?*

"A sign? What kind of sign?" I asked.

"The proof that God is real."

He walked toward me. Instinctively, I raised the gun, but he kept coming. Our eyes met, and no fear was in his, only love, kindness, mercy. When he reached me, he took the gun gently from my hand and set it aside.

At that moment, I was totally vulnerable.

Surrendered.

If he was tricking me, then I was resigned to my fate. I lowered my head and let my shoulders sag.

He's touching my face.

His hands were soft, smooth, not calloused but strong. Startled, I pulled back slightly.

A sudden bright light erupted on my left side. Scales fell from my eye, and I could suddenly see him clearly out of my left eye. My eyes met his again. He nodded slowly. My right eye reflexively closed as I saw his hand move toward it. When I opened my right eye, I could see. Perfectly. Completely healed.

Both eyes were.

Without hesitation, his hands went to my left arm. I wanted to pull it away, but he was oblivious to my commands. His cool touch was like a salve.

How can I feel his touch? That's impossible.

His hand moved slowly from my wrist up to my shoulder. As he passed over an area, the burned and charred skin was miraculously replaced by new skin right before my eyes.

Impulsively, I wanted to reach for him, but his strength held me back as he continued to touch areas still in need of healing. My side, leg, thigh, and hip all miraculously healed as I let out squeals of delight.

Finished, his hand finally came to rest on my shoulder. "God said to tell you that he has a plan for you."

I fell to my knees, thanking God. Sobbing uncontrollably.

* * *

For the first time in three hundred years, I stepped outside the spacecraft, running around jumping, dancing, laughing, and prancing like a little kid. Elias joined in my celebrating, easily matching me step for step. When I stopped to catch my breath, he was barely breathing hard at all. After what seemed like an hour of pure fun and joy, we went back inside to get something to eat and drink.

I had so many questions for him.

"Does this planet have a name?" I asked.

"This planet is called Adon which means 'The owner is God.'"

"What's wrong?" Elias asked. He must have seen the disappointed look on my face.

"On earth, we get to name the planets we discover. Since I discovered this one, I thought I might get to name it after me. Looks like God has already named it. We should stick with his name. I like it better."

Elias laughed heartily and I joined him.

"Would you like to meet God?" he asked in no more than a casual tone.

"You mean in person?"

"Yes. I can take you to meet God."

"Are you serious? God's here on this planet?"

My belief in God was secure. No doubt in my mind that God existed. Even so, I thought God was in outer space somewhere, and we couldn't see him nor hear him speak.

"Yes. He comes to the Garden of Eden every day," Elias explained. "We can meet him there in the cool of the evening."

"The Garden of Eden is on this planet?" I asked, not fully believing what I was hearing.

Elias nodded. I stood and bolted back outside, looking at the glow over the mountain. He followed me out.

"Where's the garden?" I asked while gazing at the glow, certain it must be there.

Elias pointed that direction and said, "It's just over that hill. Not very far from here."

My hands were shaking from disbelief. The Bible had a story about a Garden of Eden on Earth, but I always thought it was a myth, a fairy tale, a figment of a writer's imagination. Apparently, one existed on this planet. If Elias was to be believed, the garden of Eden was real and not imagined.

Maybe it really existed on earth as well.

"I'm confused," I said. "There was a Garden of Eden on earth. Is this the same one?"

We headed back inside.

"It's not the same one," Elias explained. "Over the centuries, God created many planets, including Earth. He placed on each planet, a garden that he called Eden, a couple who he named Adam and Eve, and a tree of the knowledge of good and evil. On every planet except Adon, Adam and Eve ate from the tree and brought sin and death to their world."

I was riveted to every word.

"All the desolate planets in your solar system had life on them at one time," he continued. "Mercury, Mars, Venus, Jupiter, Saturn, Neptune, Uranus, Pluto, all had life on them many years ago. Every Adam and Eve ate from the tree and eventually destroyed themselves, just as earth has now destroyed itself."

"How do you know so much about earth?" I asked.

"God sent an angel to tell me all of these things so I could instruct you on the truths of the universe."

I told Elias all about earth and my journey to Adon. He was fascinated by the Bible as I opened it, and we read together the story of Adam and Eve in the Garden of Eden. Elias confirmed that it matched the story of Adon, except Adam and Eve didn't eat from the tree of the knowledge of good and evil on Adon. The garden still existed, and sin and death hadn't entered Adon like it had on earth.

"Adam and Eve are very much alive. You can meet them," Elias said.

"When can we go see the garden and meet them?" I asked excitedly.

"Right now, if you're ready. We can't see God until later today, but I can show you the garden, and we'll find Adam and Eve. They'll be around somewhere."

My hands came together in a loud crescendo as the intensity of the moment hit me. The mission had been about discovery and the search for intelligent life in outer space. Never in my wildest dreams did I ever expect to find intelligent life, much less be on the verge of finding God himself. The origins of life were within the grasp of my understanding.

I looked at myself in the mirror. *If I was going to meet God, and Adam and Eve, it wasn't going to be looking like this.*

"I'm going to take a shower and change my clothes," I told Elias. "Make yourself at home."

After a shower and a shave, I looked and felt much better. My clothes went on much easier than they had a few hours before. My wounds were completely healed as if they'd never happened.

The robot was secured back in place, no longer needed. I couldn't help but think how close I came to cutting off my arm. I shuddered at the thought. It had to somehow be God's timing.

I can't wait to thank God in person for healing me.

We prepared to leave. Elias encouraged me to leave the door open to let the breeze inside to air out the spacecraft. My first thought was that he had people hiding in the wings who were going to loot my ship as soon as we left.

"Can I trust you... I mean... Are my things safe?" I said, immediately regretting it. I mentally slapped myself in the face as I realized how foolish it sounded.

After all Elias had done for me, I still doubted him. That was going to take some getting used to. My attitude needed to change. No need to project on this planet the insecurities and failures of my own.

He didn't seem hurt or the least bit defensive.

I explained how rampant crime and violence were on earth.

"Nothing like that would ever happen on Adon," he explained. "It's perfectly safe to leave your door open. Everybody does it. No one would ever even think to bother something that belonged to someone else."

Years away from earth had not rid me of the cynicism that had followed me from my corrupt and sinful planet. Things were different here, as I was quickly discovering.

Elias explained more things as we walked.

"Tell me about yourself," I asked.

"I'm married, with a bunch of kids. I lost count of how many a long time ago."

"How old are you?"

"I'm a little over three thousand years old."

"What?" I couldn't believe what I was hearing. I thought I was old. He listened intently as I explained that most people only lived an average of seventy-two years on earth.

"No one dies on Adon," Elias said. "Adam and Eve are over six thousand years old."

I stopped to savor the moment. For Elias, this was simply home. For me, this was the most significant historical event in the history of mankind.

"Here it is," Elias said.

"Is this the entrance to the Garden of Eden?"

"No. This is the entrance to the city. The garden is in the middle of the city."

No gate, sign, or armed guards were present as we approached the perfectly manicured entrance. As we passed through the entryway, a short path led us to a hill that overlooked the most beautiful sight my eyes had ever laid eyes on.

I gasped.

The only way to describe it was that the Emerald City in the *Wizard of Oz* paled in comparison. Adon was awash in contrasting colors seemingly in a competition for which could be the most brilliant. The city contained houses, roads, buildings, and parks. Everything was polished and pristine: windows shone like crystal reflecting light off each other. Every lawn was perfectly manicured, and thousands of colorful flowers adorned each.

The lack of skyscrapers or tall buildings was stark against the sky so blue I couldn't think of a name for it. No potholes, graffiti, trash, dead trees, or weeds were anywhere the eye could see. Everywhere was sheer perfection. Elias told me some of the houses and buildings were thousands of years old. That was hard to believe. We came down the hill and the city was more spectacular the closer we got.

Men, women, and children were walking, playing, and riding their own version of bicycles, laughing, and having a good time. Some were working, but they seemed to be enjoying their work. Most took time to acknowledge us. Elias waved and smiled to each one as if he knew everybody.

We came around a corner, and a tiger suddenly bounded out of the trees and ran straight toward us.

"Elias, run!" I turned to run away, but Elias grabbed my arm.

The tiger ran right up to my feet and stopped. It had a ball in his mouth.

"He wants to play with you," Elias said.

The tiger dropped the ball and jumped around like a dog wanting to play fetch.

"Pick up the ball and throw it."

The tiger bounced after the ball excitedly. A few seconds later, the toy was back at my feet. I threw it again. This time the tiger got distracted and headed straight for some kids playing in a park. It jumped on one of the kids, knocking him to the ground.

A surge of panic coursed through my veins. I ran as fast as I could to help the little boy.

As I got closer, I could see that the kid was laughing as he and the tiger playfully wrestled on the ground.

"Look over there," Elias said. He pointed to something to my right.

Two kids, a boy and a girl, barely four years old, were sitting on top of a crocodile, riding it across a lawn. The croc had his mouth wide open in a huge grin.

My mouth stayed as open as the croc's as I saw lions, bears, elephants, giraffes, zebras, moose, and many other animals too numerous to count. In the middle of the city was a large lake where hippos, seals, and water buffaloes were splashing around. Adults and kids swam nearby with no concern whatsoever for their safety.

We turned on a street with houses made of shimmering crystal, each one unique in their own way, but each blending in unity like a planned development.

Elias turned right at a street and crossed the road. We walked up a sidewalk to a house with huge double doors and an arched picture window above them. Elias walked in without knocking.

"Don't you need to knock?" I asked.

"It's not necessary. Like I said, everyone leaves their doors open."

Elias called out for Adam and Eve. Obviously, their house. No one answered, so we made our way back outside. As we were leaving, a man walked up to the house. I wondered for a moment if we were in trouble.

"Do you know where Adam and Eve are?" Elias asked the man.

"Mom and Dad are down at the café."

We weren't in trouble after all. He was perfectly friendly as if he expected to see us walking uninvited out of his parent's house.

"I would like for you to meet a good friend of mine," Elias said. "His name is Adam as well."

He reached out and shook my hand firmly.

"Pleased to me you. My name is Jezrah."

Elias said goodbye to Jezrah. They kissed on the cheeks. As we were leaving, Jezrah said, "Hey Adam. I live right across the street. Come over any time."

"Thanks. I will," I said, still trying to process how unbelievably friendly everyone was.

Elias turned to me and said, "Let's go find Adam and Eve."

Chapter Twenty

The café sat on a quaint side street backing up to a forest three short blocks from Adam and Eve's house. Patios surrounded the restaurant on both sides. Brightly colored tables and chairs were filled with patrons clearly enjoying themselves. We walked through the doorway with a sign above that read "Everyone Welcome." From my vantage point, everyone certainly seemed as if they felt welcomed.

Elias identified Adam as the man standing in the corner with a crowd of people around him, obviously hanging on his every word. We couldn't hear what he said, but everyone filled the inside of the cafe with laughter after he said it. Adam had a huge grin on his face obviously enjoying the attention.

As we made our way to that side of the cafe, the crowd parted, and I saw Eve for the first time. She turned her head slightly to look our way. It took a few seconds before I realized I'd been holding my breath, giving practical meaning to the term "breathtaking."

He has been married to her for six thousand years. I can't even imagine being married to a woman that beautiful for even one day.

Her hair was long and flowing, a rich shade of honey. Her eyes glowed a bright emerald green. Full lips. High cheekbones. Perfect features. She reached out her hand and touched mine as she stood to greet us. She smiled sweetly and softly said, "I'm Eve. It's so nice to meet you. Welcome to Adon."

Elias kissed Eve on her silky looking, smooth cheeks that shone without a single line or blemish. Every aspect of Eve competed for my attention. I caught myself staring in amazement at all of them. One would hold my amazement only until another caught my eye. I would stare at Eve's hair, then her eyes, then her cheeks, her perfectly proportioned body, and then my gaze would come back to her hair and start over again. She didn't seem to be offended.

Before my staring became too awkward, a young girl ran up to Eve waving a drawing she had obviously just created. Eve bent down and told her, "Wow! That's so good. You're so amazing." She stroked the girl's hair and said, "You're beautiful. Do you know that? Look how big you are. You're getting bigger every day." The girl beamed as she ran back to her table on the other side of the café.

Elias motioned for the crowd not to give away his presence as he came up from behind Adam as he said, "I'm made of dust, but my beautiful wife Eve is prime rib."

The group laughed with approval. Elias wrapped his arms around Adam in a big bear hug.

"How many times are you going to tell that story?" Elias asked. "I've heard it thousands of times. You need some new material." Elias poked Adam in his ribs as he said it.

"Elias, my old friend, how are you today?" Adam said.

"Who are you calling old? You're a lot older than I am," Elias said jokingly.

"Well, you're right about that," Adam said with a grin.

Elias continued the banter. "How old are you now, six thousand years?" He put his arm around Adam's shoulder. "You don't look a day over five thousand." The crowd roared with laughter. Adam and Elias kissed each other on the cheeks.

Elias turned back to the crowd and said, "Do you know what God said after he created Adam?"

Everyone listened intently.

"God said, 'I can do a lot better than this. So, he made Eve.'"

The crowd clapped in appreciation of the two friends who appeared to deeply love each other.

"You're definitely the better half," Elias said of Eve.

The crowd dispersed, and Adam and Eve invited us to join them for lunch. Word of a stranger from another planet had obviously gotten back to them and piqued their curiosity. As anxious as I was to meet them, they seemed even more excited to meet me. Although, it occurred to me they were probably like that with everyone. It didn't take long for me to determine that Adam and Eve were the nicest people I'd ever met.

Elias ordered food for everyone. Eve took my hand and held it, looking directly into my eyes. She stroked my hair and face and ran her hand up and down my arm. Nothing romantic or sexual could be inferred from the gestures. Maybe on earth, it would've seemed forward, suggestive. On Adon, it seemed as natural as shaking hands. Almost as if Eve couldn't possibly have an improper thought, motive, or gesture.

Eve could've been a mother comforting a young boy who'd fallen and scraped his knee. She must've sensed the years of pain and heartache I'd endured over the course of three hundred years alone in a spacecraft with no touch from anyone. Every stroke of her loving and gentle hands sent those hurts fleeing as my soul soaked in the intended love like a sponge soaks up water.

Eve is mesmerizing.

The four of us talked for hours. My adventures from earth were fascinating to them, and they wanted to know everything I could tell them about life on earth. I felt like the only person in the room, the center of their focus. Like they'd known me all my life even though we'd just met.

Eve was warm and friendly, Adam funny and personable. Together, they seemed inseparable. Two parts of one whole. They looked at each other with smiles and glances only two people deeply in love could share. More than once, I caught their private looks of love and adoration. Every few minutes, they reached out and touched each other in a loving and familiar way, seemingly not wanting to let much time pass between expressions of love for each other. Six thousand years had only increased their commitment and desire. An amazing love story was the only way to describe it.

"What does a man give his wife for his six thousandth year anniversary?" I asked Adam, jokingly.

They didn't seem to get my joke. Some things never changed even on a different planet. No one on Earth got my jokes either.

I explained that on Earth twenty-five was a silver anniversary and gold was a fifty-year anniversary and that couples exchanged gifts on those special occasions. Once they understood, they replied that God always gave them everything they needed. They didn't have to give each other gifts. Having God and each other was all they needed to be happy.

The conversation took a serious turn when I shared with them the story of Adam and Eve and how they ate the fruit from the tree on earth. I explained how Adam and Eve's sin on earth had led to wars, crime, death, and even the destruction of the earth through a flood.

When I shared about the messages I had received about the destruction of earth at the final battle, Eve laid her head on her husband's shoulder.

"That could have been us," she said.

"How did you keep from eating from the tree of the knowledge of good and evil?" I asked. "Of all the planets, you're the only two people who were able to resist the temptation."

Eve looked at Adam, waiting for him to speak. He nodded as if to tell her to share the story.

"I almost did."

She spoke in a slow and careful manner almost in a whisper.

Her eyes narrowed, and she looked away momentarily, obviously remembering.

"We lived in the garden. God wasn't there that afternoon. The serpent came to the garden fairly often, but we always avoided him. He gave me a chilling feeling every time I saw him. That day, he came right up to me. Usually when the serpent tried to talk to me, I just ran away. I should've run away that day, but Adam was nearby tending to the garden, so I thought I was safe."

She paused and her body shook in a shudder. Even though six thousand years had passed, she related it like it had happened yesterday.

"The serpent tried to trick me into eating the fruit off the tree. He said I could be like God. The serpent said it so convincingly, for a moment I believed him. He led me over to the fruit and tried to get me to eat it."

She paused, letting the words sink in.

"I started to call for Adam, but I didn't. I should have."

"But you didn't eat the fruit. Why not?" I asked.

"I reached for it. I started to take it. My hand touched it. I started to put it to my mouth."

Eve dropped her head but then looked up quickly. "He said something I knew was a lie," she said excitedly.

"What did he say," I asked, mesmerized by the story.

"He said..."

Her voice quivered.

"Go ahead and eat it. God said you would die if you touched the fruit. You just touched it and you didn't die."

The pace of her words quickened. "God never said that. He said we would die if we ate the fruit. He never said we would die if we touched it. I knew at that moment that the serpent was lying to me. I screamed and Adam came running. He told the serpent to leave me alone. The serpent started yelling at me. He bowed up on his hind legs and spread his arms like he was going to attack us. Adam stood between the serpent and me. At first, the serpent wouldn't leave. Adam stepped toward him. He was so brave."

"What happened next?" I asked.

"We heard God walking around in the garden and the serpent took off immediately."

Adam interjected, "She was so strong. I'm proud of her. I don't think I would've been able to withstand the temptation. But she did it."

Eve nodded. "I remembered how good God had always been to me. He gave me a wonderful husband. An amazing life. I love God so much. I didn't want to let him down. I didn't realize at the time how I would have been letting everyone down..."

The realization of the consequences of eating the fruit were obviously hitting her.

"When you describe what Earth has gone through," Eve said sorrowfully. "I can't imagine. What if I'd been responsible for all that pain and heartache for everyone? It would've been awful. I don't know how I could've lived with myself."

"I would be dead. We would all be dead. Everyone would be dead." she said. Tears welled up in her eyes, bringing out even more of her beauty. It seemed impossible that she could seem even more beautiful.

She composed herself. "The serpent hasn't bothered me since, not once even after all these years." Eve said the words with resolve, almost angrily.

Elias said, "The serpent still tries to get someone to eat the fruit. No one will do it. We owe that to the two of you. Your example has let us withstand the serpent for six thousand years. Thank you. Everyone in Adon thanks you. We all owe you a huge debt of gratitude."

Eve turned and looked at me with piercing and determined eyes. She said, "Adam, the serpent still wants someone to eat the fruit. Be very careful. He's crafty and sly. He'll lie to you. Don't believe his lies. He'll flee from you if you resist him."

"We're going over to the garden tonight so Adam can meet God," Elias said.

The sky had darkened, and Elias explained that God came to the garden during the cool of the evening, so my excitement grew, hoping we would head over there soon.

"How is it that there is light and darkness on Adon?" I asked. "On earth, we have a sun. There's no sun here."

"God provides the light." Elias explained. "It's his glory that shines during the day. He then gives us the night so we can rest."

"I'm so glad you are going to meet God," Eve said. "God's so wonderful. You'll love meeting him."

I nodded more out of nervousness than agreement.

I asked if I could pay for the food. Their puzzled looks told me I needed to explain. The question was actually a foolish one. I didn't have any money and no way to pay for the check even if they'd let me.

"We don't pay for our food on Adon. God provides everything we need," Elias explained. "The people running the café do so to help others. It's their calling. It's what they love to do. No one ever pays for anything. If someone needs something, we just give it to them."

The café served the most amazing food. Three hundred years of eating food from packets would have made any food taste good. Still, the café food tasted better than anything I'd ever eaten in my entire life. Better than the best restaurants on earth by far. Knowing the food was free made it even better.

What an unbelievable place. Can it get any better than this?

* * *

As we left the café, Eve took my hand, and we started running. Several children joined us. We laughed, jumped, and danced as we made our way across the city. I felt like a kid again. When it was time to leave, Adam and Eve both kissed me on the cheeks and told me to stop by their house any time I wanted and that I was always welcome there.

Elias and I set out walking. Some of the kids followed us, still laughing and playing. A few wild animals joined in the fun. We rounded a curve, and everyone stopped.

Just ahead was a lavish entrance.

The Garden of Eden.

Two angels stood at the gate. I approached the entrance cautiously.

"The angels are here. That means God is here already," Elias said. "Adam take off your shoes. We're about to enter holy ground."

I slipped off my shoes and put them in my backpack. Elias didn't wear shoes.

We walked right past the two angels.

"Don't we have to stop at the gate? Won't the guards stop us?" I asked.

"They're not guards. They're cherubim angels who stand at the entrance whenever God's in the garden. Everyone can enter the garden at any time, even when God is here. The angels leave when God leaves."

"Is God in there right now?"

"Yes. God's somewhere walking in the garden."

Fear gripped me, and I began to shake.

"Don't be afraid." Elias must have sensed it because he said, "Just enter his presence with thanksgiving. You are thankful for what God did for you yesterday aren't you?"

"Very much so."

"Then you'll be fine."

Elias took off walking briskly. I tried to keep up, hardly believing I was about to enter the Garden of Eden.

* * *

For a moment, neither of us spoke.

I expected the garden to be dark, like walking in a forest. Instead, I found lights, beautiful bright lights, colors everywhere. My senses couldn't process everything.

A hundred different fragrances stirred my senses with every breath. Jasmine, ginger, honeysuckle, and mint among others. A smorgasbord of colors mixed together to form a radiant display. Red and purples, green and reds, lavender and pinks, orange and blues. The colors adorned every tree, flower, and bush. I wanted to roll around on the perfectly manicured, lush green, grassy areas.

Sounds reverberated through the garden like a shout in a canyon. Birds chirped in unison as butterflies and hummingbirds flitted their way from flower to flower. A butterfly landed on my shoulder and then flew away, leaving a smile on my face.

A brook curved its way through the garden fed by a small water-fall cascading over the rock of a small cliff. Tall oak trees dominated the sky as if they were in charge and were guarding the garden. A cool mist permeated the air.

Elias walked over to a tree and pulled off a piece of fruit and handed it to me. He motioned for me to take a bite. I bit into it and my mouth exploded with sensations. The texture surprised me. Silky, not crunchy or hard like an apple on Earth. Smooth, enticing, each bite left me wanting more. Each bite was different than the ones before. Almost like a box of chocolates I remembered eating as a child, a surprise filling in each piece.

We continued strolling through the garden, taking in the sights. Several animals were wandering about, although not as many as on the outside. People milled around, clearly enjoying the atmosphere.

A couple sat in a perfectly manicured park-like area having a picnic. Another man sang and played an instrument. A few people seemed to be praying. One man lay on the ground sleeping.

We rounded a corner and two magnificent trees came into view. My mouth gaped in awe. A river separated us from the trees perched on a small hill directly across from us.

"Those are the tree of life and the tree of the knowledge of good and evil," Elias explained.

He didn't have to tell me; I already knew. The trees weren't as large as I expected but more colorful and beautiful than my mind had imagined. The trees stood on the bank of a pond fed by one river which Elias explained flowed from the sea of Adonai.

The pond divided into four branches and flowed throughout the entire garden, providing water for the plants and trees. I could see gold and onyx stones in the rivers. I reached down and took one of the stones from the water. The water was warm and refreshing. The bottom and top of the stone were perfectly smooth. It brought back memories of the stones I skipped across the surface of a lake back on earth, except that these stones were like jewels.

Elias didn't speak but let me take in the reverence of the moment.

Sometime later he said, "God has told us that we may freely eat the fruit of every tree in the garden except this one." He pointed to the tree of the knowledge of good and evil. God said that we can't eat the fruit of that tree or we will die."

The tree of life stood further away on a hill behind the tree of the knowledge of good and evil and was much more difficult to get to.

The two trees kept my focus as I stared in wonder. The Bible had a phrase "the fear of the Lord." I understood better what it meant. Fear, not in the sense of being afraid; rather a reverence for God. No one could experience the awesomeness of the garden and not be in reverence of God.

A cool breeze swept through the garden, and I heard someone walking.

"What was that?" I whispered.

"You don't have to whisper. That's God," Elias said with a wide grin.

I listened intently. When I heard the sound again, I said these words, "Thank you, God, for healing me." They barely came out of my mouth and my voice quivered as I said them. I looked to Elias, not sure what to do next.

I wondered if God had heard me.

Then I heard a still, small voice clearly say, "Here am I." Not an audible voice, but something deep inside of me. Something unmistakable. The voice of God.

The breeze stopped as quickly as it had come. I could no longer hear any movement, no more rustling.

"He's gone," Elias said. "The cherubim are gone as well. It's time for us to go."

We began walking back.

More movement. A large shadow. An eerie presence.

Elias grabbed my hand and said, "Quick. Come this way."

I looked back and saw a large serpent. It had a long, thick head, like a giraffe with a large body, and a long, skinny tail. It looked like a cross between a snake, giraffe, and a dinosaur.

"Don't look back. Keep moving." Elias didn't seem to be afraid, but I could sense urgency in his voice.

We exited the garden to a loud, menacing, and evil roar.

"What was that?" I asked.

"That was the devil. Be careful and keep an eye out for him. He wants to kill, steal, and destroy everything you have."

"Can he harm me?"

"Only if you let him. He has no authority to do anything to you.

Don't be afraid of him, just be on the lookout. He walks around Adon looking for someone to devour. We just ignore him. He has no power over us. Just be aware."

"I will."

I hope I never see him again.

Chapter Twenty-One

Four months later

I *feel like I'm a good person trapped in a body with a bad person.* Or maybe it's the other way around.

I was alone on the observation deck, overwhelmed by my feelings and thoughts.

Lately, I found myself spending less and less time in the city of Adon. The people there just reminded me of how imperfect I am. It's not their fault. They've been really good to me. We're just different.

It's not them, it's me.

Elias invited me to spend a week as a guest at his home. His wife and kids were wonderful people who treated me like royalty the entire week. The home cooked meals were amazing, and the week was the most stress-free I'd ever experienced in my life.

But the whole time they were obsessed with God. They literally lived and breathed God, twenty-four seven. God was all they talked about nonstop.

I understood. God had been good to them. They had a perfect life all because of God.

"Don't get me wrong," I said aloud even though no one could hear me. "I want to be just like them. I just can't be."

I'm not a good enough person to be around these people for very long.

I've tried to be. I read through the Bible three times over the past four months. I devoured it front to back like a hungry bear would devour a prey after hibernating for the winter. While I understood the Bible somewhat, the people of Adon wouldn't. There's no way they could.

They have no idea what life is like in the real world.

They were too sheltered. God protected them from everything. A fire like what I had on Chronos could never happen here. God would put it out before it ever got started and certainly before it hurt someone.

I considered writing down my thoughts, but instead just let them come unhindered.

That's wonderful that God has been so good to them. But how does someone like me fit in? A fire could break out in my spacecraft, and I don't know if God would put it out for me or not. I'm not as good as these people. I don't live and breathe God twenty-four seven like they do.

I resent that everyone's so perfect here. They're always happy, always content. I'm not always happy, not always content. In fact, I'm unhappy a lot. Sad a lot. Angry a lot.

What brought this to a head was something that happened this afternoon.

I was sitting by the lake reading a book, minding my own business. Some kids were playing, and they threw a ball, knocking over my drink. I yelled at them and threw their ball into the lake.

Why did I do that? I felt so ashamed. They were just kids. Why was I so angry? What did I have to be angry about?

The kids didn't even notice. They just went into the lake and got their ball back. They didn't even know that I'd done something bad to them. They were laughing and playing as if nothing had happened.

I wish I could be that way. I really do. But I'm not.

I'm afraid a lot. Seeing a tiger running toward me still scares me. I worry about walking back to the spacecraft alone at night. That's stupid. I'm perfectly safe.

The people of Adon aren't afraid of anything.

I'm afraid I'm going to be alone for the rest of my life. That's my biggest fear.

I'm sorry, but I'm jealous of Adam. I wish I had a wife like Eve. I think about her a lot at night right before I go to sleep. I try to put those thoughts out of my head, but I wish she was lying next to me. I hate that I think about her in that way. She's been so good to me. So has Adam. I love them so much

I'm such a horrible person.

There's no way any of the girls on Adon are ever going to be interested in me. I have no future with them. We're too different. They could never love me. I'm too imperfect.

I'm divorced.

No one on Adon has ever been divorced before. Every relationship is completely pure. It would never be pure with me. I have a past. I have memories.

My sorrows consume me sometimes.

I have a lot of losses. A lot of death to remember.

No one has ever died on Adon. Everyone I loved on earth is dead.

They've never experienced that kind of loss. They couldn't understand how painful it was. They'll never die.

After reading the Bible, I think I understand it.

I know the difference between good and evil. They don't. That's what happened at the fall. That's why it's called the fall. I fell from what God wanted for me. We all did.

They never fell. They only know what is good. All they know is a good God. They don't know a God who's angry. I would give anything to only know what is good, to only know God's love.

I feel guilty even thinking about these things.

I feel bad that I yelled at those kids.

I need to go apologize.

* * *

I left the spacecraft and went back to Adon. I searched everywhere for the kids, but they weren't anywhere to be found. I wandered around somewhat in a daze, mostly just feeling sorry for myself.

I went into the Garden of Eden and laid down and cried. The garden always made me feel better. Today it didn't.

A small groundhog came up to me and started licking away my tears. I swatted it away.

Why would I do that? That's my dilemma. The little groundhog was just trying to make me feel better, and that's how I treated him. He didn't deserve that. I immediately felt bad.

Sitting in the garden, it started to make sense to me. The difference between the people of Adon and me was the crown of glory that God had put on them. Psalm 8:5 described it. When God created Adam and Eve, he made them a little lower than the angels and with a crown of glory. That crown didn't allow them to see or know evil. The Adam and Eve on Earth lost that crown when they sinned. The people of Adon never lost it. They were oblivious to evil.

The crown was the glow, the aura, that was around them. The reason they were naked but not ashamed. They didn't need clothes. They were covered by that crown.

A thought occurred to me.

What if God gave me that crown?

The thought excited me. *Is it possible?*

Nothing was impossible for God. I read that in the Bible.

If God would put that crown on me, then I could be just like the people of Adon. I could be sinless again like them. The anger would leave. So would the sadness, fear, and jealousy. Maybe a woman would want to marry me. We could have kids together. I would never die.

I was so excited I could hardly stand it. I decided to come back to the garden in the evening and ask God to restore that crown for me. Night hadn't yet fallen, and God wouldn't be in the garden for several hours. I headed back to my spacecraft to eat something and to get ready.

I rushed over the hill and down to my spacecraft.

I ran up the ramp and stopped. I suddenly felt a presence in the room.

Sitting in my chair was a woman.

"Hi Adam. I'm Lucy," she said.

* * *

"Lucy, we thought you were dead!" I couldn't believe what I was seeing.

"As you can see, I'm very much alive." She smiled at me in a sly, cute way.

I wasn't sure how to react. I wanted to run to her, grab her, and give her a hug, but we'd just met. I didn't know what was appropriate.

Instead, I said, "I'm so glad you're here. Are you okay?"

"I'm okay. My spacecraft crashed a couple miles from here."

"It crashed?" I said with alarm in my voice.

'Not really crashed. Just a hard landing. Everything's okay, but I won't be flying it anywhere anytime soon."

"I don't think either of us are going anywhere. I have so much to tell you."

Getting a read on Lucy was hard. She was different in a way that I couldn't figure out. I knew her back at NASA, but that was more than three hundred years ago. The memory of her had faded. She didn't look or sound the same for some reason.

Lucy was medium height and slender, had a curvy figure in a sexy way, clearly flaunting it but not overly so. She wore a tank top and short shorts. The shirt wasn't long enough to cover her well-toned stomach. She wasn't as beautiful as Eve, but no one was. If Eve was a ten, Lucy was an eight.

On earth, Lucy would be the prettiest girl in most rooms. Her eyes were mysterious, maybe even mischievous, devilish, yet they were alluring, enticing.

"How did you find me?" I asked.

"I got your message. You said to stop by any time. Is now a good time?" she said with a big grin on her face.

I laughed. "Now is a good time, but you should've called first. The place is a mess. I haven't had time to clean it up. I wasn't expecting company."

Lucy laughed and I was hooked. It could be the fact that I hadn't been close to a woman of my own ilk in three hundred years. Maybe my normal male hormones were roaring back to life. Lucy had been there less than ten minutes, and I was already falling for her.

"Were you married on earth?" I wanted to kick myself as soon as I asked the question. *What a dumb question to ask right away.*

Of course, she wasn't married. She wouldn't have been considered for the program if she'd had a family. I hoped I wasn't being too obvious or too forward. If I was, Lucy didn't seem to mind.

"I've never been married. I've been married to space travel all my life."

"Me too. I know what you mean. I was married before, but she died." My voice trailed off.

I didn't feel the need to explain further. It wasn't exactly a lie, but it wasn't exactly the truth either. I would just leave it at that. I wondered why I was so nervous around her. We just met, and I was acting like a silly schoolboy.

I'd always been nervous around women on earth. Apparently, being three hundred years older didn't make it any easier for me to talk to women, even on a totally different planet. Old behaviors had a way of resurfacing as I was finding out in real time.

I changed the subject. "Where are you from?"

"I grew up in Salem, Massachusetts. I went to school at Boston College. How about you?"

I didn't notice an accent. I made a note to ask her about that later.

"Charlottesville, Virginia. My parents died when I was young. I didn't have any brothers or sisters. I was always fascinated with the stars and planets. My mom got me a telescope for my ninth birthday, and I was hooked."

"Chemistry set for me. I had the set for two weeks, almost blew the house up, and they took it away from me. But I was hooked too. I couldn't get enough of chemistry, physics, math, and science. Those were what I loved the most. My sister and I used to sneak out of the house at night and look at the stars, and I told her one night that I was going to be an astronaut."

She shrugged her shoulders. "And here I am."

I was surprised she mentioned a sister. I thought the criteria for the program was you had to be an only child and didn't have any family. They must have made an exception for her, or maybe her sister had died. I didn't want to press the subject.

"I thought you were further behind me. How did you get here so fast?"

"I don't know. Maybe my craft was faster."

This time, Lucy changed the subject, "Do you have something to eat? I'm starving."

"Sure, let me get you something." All I had to offer her was the same thing she'd been eating for three hundred years. I would've loved to take her to the café, but it was already closed.

What did she mean about the spacecraft being faster?

That was impossible. I dismissed the thought. I didn't really care how she got here quicker; I was ecstatic that she was.

"Do you feel like Italian, Chinese, or American food tonight?" I asked.

It was all the same food in one little pill but had flavorings added to make it whatever you wanted it to be.

"Surprise me."

Lucy walked up behind me and put her arms around my waist. Her hair brushed against my neck, and I felt chills go up and down my spine. No doubt about it; love at first sight.

* * *

Three hours later, we had our first fight.

It wasn't really a fight. I said the wrong thing, and Lucy reacted angrily. I was telling Lucy all about the city of Adon and the garden. When I mentioned introducing her to everyone, she got defensive.

"I don't want to meet them yet," she insisted.

"Why not?"

"Do I have to have a reason?" she said sharply.

"You'll love them. I can show you around, and we can eat at this great café. Don't you want to meet Adam and Eve? I know where they live, and I can introduce you to them."

"I don't want to meet Adam and Eve," Lucy said almost with animosity in her voice.

I should've let it go, but I didn't.

"You don't have to meet anyone if you don't want to. Let me show you around, though. We can go there in the morning. It's the most beautiful place you'll ever see."

"I said that I didn't want to go. Just drop it." she said angrily. "I'm going to leave."

She got up to go.

"Don't go. I'm sorry. I won't bring it up again," I said.

"It's late. I'm going back to my spacecraft. It was nice to meet you," she said matter-of-factly.

"At least let me walk you back to your ship."

"That's silly. It's two miles away. I'll be fine."

"No, I insist. I want to go with you."

"Adam, I want to be alone," she said sternly. "I'll see you tomorrow."

And then she was gone. As quickly as she had entered my life, she'd left it. Not for good, but it was a weird enough exchange to give me pause.

"What was wrong with her? What had I said that was so bad? Why didn't she want to meet the people of Adon? That's what she traveled all this way for."

Many questions were pulsing through my mind.

I watched her walk away until she was out of view. Maybe she needed time. Adjusting to life on Adon took some getting used to as I knew firsthand. Things were happening too fast. Three hundred years alone in a spacecraft would mess anyone up. She was amazing. She would be fine.

In my excitement, I'd pushed her too hard. I was going to need to give her time and space. On Adon, we had all the time in the world. We weren't going anywhere, anytime soon.

* * *

Lucy didn't come the next day. I sat on the observation deck all day waiting for her.

What did I say that was so bad? I just wanted to introduce her to my friends.

I would apologize when I saw her, but I wasn't sure I'd done anything wrong. I'd never been good with women. Apparently, I hadn't gotten better at understanding women three hundred years later.

I put on hold the plan to ask God for the crown. If I got the crown, I wouldn't have a future with Lucy unless she got one too. I wanted to see where the relationship went first.

The next morning, I saw Lucy well before she saw me. I ran out of the spacecraft and walked toward her.

When Lucy saw me, she ran toward me. She threw her arms around my neck, jumped into my arms, wrapped her legs around my waist, and kissed me on the lips. I wasn't expecting it, and it took a moment for me to get my bearings enough to kiss her back. By the time I did, the kiss was over.

I started to say something, but Lucy interrupted me and said, "I'm so sorry. I didn't mean to be so short with you. Will you forgive me?"

"Of course. It was my fault anyway. Take all the time you need. I'm here for you. We won't go to Adon until you're ready."

"Do you want to go on a picnic with me?" she asked.

"Are you asking me on a date?"

"Do you want it to be a date?"

"Maybe I do. We'll see."

Lucy took off running toward the spacecraft, and said, "I'll race you."

That day went much better.

* * *

For the next week, we were inseparable. Except at night. Lucy always insisted on going back to her spacecraft at night. We almost had another spat when I wanted to go back with her, but she wouldn't let me. I didn't understand why she wouldn't tell me where her spacecraft was and why she wouldn't let me go back there with her.

Safety wasn't my concern. I mostly wanted to keep her company. She thought it foolish for me to walk two miles there and two miles back. When I pressed the subject, she would get defensive and angry. So, I dropped it.

I resigned myself to the fact that I wasn't going to go to her place until she wanted me to. I thought maybe she wanted to maintain her independence. She wanted her own place for the time being, and I needed to respect that. I thought about following her one night, but if I did and she found out about it, I knew she would be furious. Lucy had a temper. Things were going too well to risk it.

We went on more picnics together, took long walks, and sat on the observation deck for hours talking. We listened to music together and even had our first dance. The kisses were growing more and more intense as time went on. Lucy was taking things somewhat slowly from a physical standpoint, but she was very passionate, and I was mesmerized with every touch.

Mostly, we talked. The conversation generally went well until I brought up something about Earth. She obviously didn't want to talk about home, and she almost always changed the subject.

I could talk about myself, but she wouldn't fully answer questions about herself. She was evasive and avoided details. I was convinced there was something she wasn't telling me. I surmised she'd signed up for the program because she was running from something in her past she wanted to forget. I decided not to press the subject.

I had my own hurts from Earth that I wanted to forget. She obviously had her own demons.

* * *

I was surprised later that evening when Lucy said, "I want to see the garden."

"Great. I'll take you there tomorrow morning."

"No. I want to go when nobody's there. Didn't you say that everyone is asleep at night? Let's go now when we won't run into anybody."

I started to ask why she didn't want to run into anyone, but I knew that was a touchy subject and decided not to go there.

"It's not a far walk. Come on, Adam." Lucy implored.

I wasn't sure how Lucy knew it wasn't a very far walk. Maybe she'd already gone there herself at night, or maybe I'd mentioned it wasn't very far and didn't remember. Anyway, I was excited she finally wanted to go.

"I'm kind of tired tonight," I said. "It's been a long day. Can we go tomorrow night?" We were snuggling in the spacecraft, and I wasn't looking forward to going out again.

"Please Adam. I'll make it worth your while." Lucy planted a long and deep kiss on me. I knew we were going to the garden.

"I don't want to be seen. Can you make sure nobody sees us?"

She was strange and mysterious, but I was madly in love with her. By that point, I would do anything she said.

* * *

We didn't have to do much sneaking around. Everyone was asleep. Elias had said everyone slept soundly at night. No one had nightmares, no one experienced restless nights, and everyone had a peaceful night's sleep. They all left their doors unlocked at night, and many left their windows up so they could sleep with the cool night air.

We wouldn't be seen, but we had to be quiet or we'd run the risk of waking someone. I wasn't sure why Lucy was so afraid of meeting anyone, but I wanted to protect her and make sure we didn't.

The night air was cool. Not too cold, but enough for a jacket. The cool air was refreshing and invigorating. I couldn't get over how the climate was perfect all the time. Never too hot and never too cold.

No guards stood in front of the entrance to the garden, so I knew God wasn't there. Lucy gave no response as we approached. I was astonished the first time I saw the entrance.

She walked right in like she knew where she was going.

"Lucy, you need to take off your shoes," I yelled trying to get her attention. She kept going. Either she didn't hear me, or she ignored what I said.

I struggled to keep up. We had the garden all to ourselves. Lucy amazed me with her confidence and willingness to walk right into the garden like she belonged.

I admired her from a distance as I watched her make her way. It'd been a whirlwind romance. I could tell that she'd fallen for me as well. While she had her quirks, I was convinced she was the girl I was going to marry. I couldn't wait to introduce her to Adam and Eve. I wasn't sure when Lucy would let that happen but was sure she would eventually.

I kept a watchful eye out for the serpent. Elias said he couldn't hurt me unless I let him, but I wasn't taking any chances. I would protect Lucy with my life. Lucy said she wasn't afraid of the serpent, and she wasn't acting like she was.

For a moment, I wasn't sure where she went. I stepped around a corner and saw her wading across the stream. Panic struck as I saw her walking toward the tree of the knowledge of good and evil.

"Lucy, come back." I said. "You're not allowed over there."

"Adam. Come on. It's beautiful over here."

"God said we're not allowed over there."

"That's not what he said. He said you couldn't eat from the tree. He didn't say you couldn't look at it."

"Come on Adam. Come and give me a kiss."

I waded across the water. I waited for the kiss, but Lucy was already over by the tree. "Lucy don't touch the tree. God said if you touch it you will die."

Lucy ignored me, "Look, Adam. I touched it and I didn't die."

Lucy gave me the fruit. I couldn't believe I was holding it. It did look good. I remembered how wonderful the fruit was that I ate with Elias. This looked even better.

"Come on Adam. You can eat it. You won't die."

I stood for a moment, holding the fruit.

"Adam, eat it," Lucy said, "and then let's go make love in the garden. I want our first time to be here. Do this for me."

I took a bite.

EPILOGUE

"For if by the one man's offense (Adam) many died, much more the grace of God and the gift by the grace of the one Man, Jesus Christ, abounded to many." Romans 5:17 (Parenthesis added)

Chapter Twenty-Two

Lucy's body began to tremble. Her mouth elongated. Contorted. Fangs began to protrude from her mouth.

What's happening? Adam threw the fruit to the ground and strained his eyes, trying to process what he was seeing.

Fire spewed from Lucy's mouth, dripping like saliva down her chin onto the ground.

Adam moved toward her, wanting to somehow save her.

Save her from what?

Her body began to morph. She suddenly stood twenty feet tall. Her arms transformed into wings. Flailing the wings from side to side, she molted her skin away like a snake.

Her eyes became like burning coals—red, ablaze with fury. The eyes that moments before looked at Adam longingly, lovingly, enticing him to eat the fruit so they could make love now became a raging inferno of hate.

Her chest pulsated as slimy green scales formed. Her fingers became bony claws with long fingernails. Her arms were swiping back and forth like they were swatting away something flying around her head.

The serpent crouched down like a tiger about to pounce on a prey. Its neck growing and protruding, getting longer.

"Lucy?" Adam instinctively reached for her as the last feature of Lucy disappeared from the serpent's body. Not fully realizing what was happening, he thought he still needed to fight for her as if the serpent had somehow consumed her against her will.

"I'm not Lucy, you fool; I'm Lucifer!" The serpent roared the words in a loud, booming, evil voice that echoed throughout the garden.

"What have I done?" Adam cried out in disbelief.

Lucifer is Satan. Lucy is the devil. No! It's not possible.

He'd been tricked.

Lucy was the devil in disguise!

Adam reached to cover his eyes, not wanting to see the evil transforming his beloved Lucy into this horrible creature. His hands shook as he staggered backward in panic. *God commanded me not to eat of the tree. Elias said to be careful. Eve warned me.*

Gurgling sounds came from the serpent's mouth, as his words mixed with a diabolical laugh. "You are a pathetic little man. You have eaten the apple, and now every world has eaten the apple—even Adon."

Satan roared with laughter. "You think I wanted to kiss you. You disgust me. I hate you. I hated every time you touched me."

Adam lunged for the serpent, but he easily evaded Adam's reach. Anger raged inside him. He wanted to kill Lucifer.

The serpent continued to taunt him. "You're a dead man. God's going to kill you. He told you if you ate of the fruit you would die. Die, Adam. Die!"

Adam's heartbeat pulsed faster and faster. "I didn't do it. You made me!" he shouted.

"You are a weak man. Just like the Adam on Earth," the serpent said accusingly. His long slimy tongue lapped up the fire that came out of his mouth with each breath. He swiped his long arm toward Adam, trying to hit him.

Adam ran and hid behind a tree.

"It's not my fault. I didn't know what I was doing," Adam said apologetically as if somehow the serpent cared.

The serpent laughed.

He continued his taunts. "I'm going to tell everyone that Adam and Eve ate the apple. They're going to finally die."

"No!" I yelled. "They had nothing to do with it. Leave them out of it."

"Eve is finally going to die. She's mocked me for all these years. Now, she's going to pay with her life."

Adam started to speak but then felt a cool breeze. The serpent immediately ran away, leaving Adam alone, cowering behind the tree.

God called out in his still small voice, "Adam, where are you?"

Adam answered, "I'm hiding over here behind the tree. I was afraid; so, I hid."

"Why were you afraid? Have you eaten from the tree I commanded you not to eat from?"

"The woman, Lucy, gave me some fruit from the tree, and I ate it." He tried to explain further, unsure if he fully understood it. "Lucy wasn't a woman at all. She was the serpent. The serpent deceived me, and I ate it."

God was furious.

Two cherubim angels suddenly appeared, holding flaming swords.

"Drive him out of the garden," God said in a loud, booming voice. "Don't let anyone in or they will eat of the tree of life and become like us."

Adam screamed in horror and began running.

The angels flew toward him and drove Adam out of the Garden of Eden. The angels stopped at the gate. They stood guard, one at each side, holding the flaming swords being brandished back and forth.

Adam ran as fast as he could back toward his spacecraft.

The people of Adon started to stir in their houses. Lights came on throughout the entire city. Several already stood on the street trying to discover the source of the commotion.

Adam slipped into the shadows, hoping no one had seen him. He avoided the houses and stayed carefully between the buildings, stealthily staying out of view as more and more townspeople came running by, all headed to the garden.

When Adam reached the top of the hill overlooking the city, he stopped to look back. Fire was coming from the garden. The ground shook. The entire city was illuminated from the fire. He heard screams and took off running again through the entrance and over the hill, not daring to look back again.

He sprinted down the hill to his spacecraft, quickly closed the door and locked himself in. Armed with weapons, he went up to the observation deck to see if anyone had followed him. A much larger glow than usual radiated in the sky over the hill.

It looked like the whole city of Adon was on fire.

Adam paced around the observation deck. He kept saying over and over again,

What have I done? What have I done?

* * *

The next morning the glow over the mountain was completely gone.

Eve sat on the back deck of her home, contemplating the unbelievable turn of events. Chaos had broken loose on Adon, and she didn't know what to do about it. Word quickly spread that someone had eaten from the tree of the knowledge of good and evil. God sealed the garden, and no one was allowed in.

Adam and I were always so careful. I need to find God, but where is he

now? Two days later, God removed the garden altogether—overnight —while everyone was sleeping. The once beautiful, majestic garden was now a barren wasteland.

Eve went to where the garden used to be and begged God to reconsider.

He wouldn't but said this to her, "Rejoice, my daughter, for a child will be born, and he will be called wonderful, counselor, mighty God, everlasting Father, and Prince of Peace. He is the Messiah and will save the people from their sins."

She told her husband, Adam, what God had said.

"What do you think it means?" Eve asked.

"I don't know, but we just have to trust God."

"Everyone now has the knowledge of good and evil," Eve said. "Before, all we saw were the good things in each other. Now everyone sees the difference between right and wrong and good and evil."

"The Adam from Earth told us this would happen."

"We can't let it happen. You and I must talk to the people. Tell them about the coming Messiah. We can't turn on each other like they did on Earth."

"We will do what we can. So many people have evil thoughts and are plotting evil things."

"God also told me that the serpent had been given authority on Adon, and he was entering into men's minds and hearts, giving them evil thoughts," Eve explained.

A sudden bang on the front door startled her. Adam stood up in his chair. A group of men entered their home.

A man named Aza faced Adam and Eve and demanded they come with him to the square to answer charges they had eaten the fruit.

Eve stood and walked over to Aza, put both hands on his shoulders, and looked directly into his eyes. "Aza, what has come over you? I was with your mother when you were born. I've watched you grow up all these years. This isn't like you."

Aza turned his head away and ordered the men to seize Adam and Eve. None of the men moved. Adam and Eve were beloved by everyone, including the men in the room.

"Word has quickly spread that you and Adam are the ones who ate the apple," one of the men said.

"Well, that's ridiculous," Adam said emphatically.

"Zelbe is inciting the crowd and making the accusations. Half the people are following her; half are on your side," the man explained.

Aza took two steps toward Eve, but Adam stood between him and Eve.

Eve raised her hand to stop Adam and said, "We'll go with you. We'll talk to the people. They know we didn't do this. Aza, you know we would have never done such a thing."

Aza glared at Eve with an evil look in his eyes.

Eve smiled and looked back at him with love.

A large crowd had gathered in the square. Zelbe stood on a platform in the middle of the throng, speaking. She had a maniacal look on her face and spoke rapidly, her hands animated with wild gestures.

What has come over Zelbe? What has come over the people of Adon? Eve needed to do something.

Zelbe waved her hands to silence the crowd. She yelled at the top of her lungs to get everyone's attention. "In every world, Adam and Eve were the ones who ate of the fruit. They have eaten the fruit on Adon, and God is mad at us. They must be punished. They must die."

Many of the people cried out, "No! Adam and Eve would never do such a thing."

Elias was there with his son Benjamin. Elias turned to Benjamin and said, "Go to the spacecraft over in Ashram. Get Adam, the man from Earth. Tell him to come quickly. Hurry. I don't know how long we can hold off this mob."

Benjamin said, "I'll tell him to bring his gun."

Eve started to object about the gun, but Benjamin had already taken off running.

Adam started to speak, but Elias stopped him. He walked up to the platform to where Zelbe stood. "You all know Adam and Eve. We all love them. They could never have done such a horrible thing."

One of the women in the crowd yelled out, "Let Adam and Eve speak for themselves."

Adam stepped from behind the throng of protection, walked up to the platform, and looked out over the crowd. Tears welled up in his eyes.

It pained Eve to see how much this was hurting her husband.

"I don't know who has eaten the fruit," he spoke calmly but with authority. "It's a terrible thing that's happened. The serpent tried to tempt us before any of you were born." Adam looked down at Eve. She nodded. "We didn't give in to the temptation, and we would not have given in to it now. It wasn't us. We were asleep in our bed."

"Did anyone see you asleep in your bed?" Zelbe said accusingly. "Let anyone come forward who can vouch for them."

Eve shouted from below the platform, "Zelbe, why have you let Satan enter your heart? You know that we haven't done this evil thing. Of course, no one would have seen us asleep in our bed. Everyone was asleep. We don't know who did this. But even if we did, they should not die. What right do you have to murder someone?"

Zelbe pointed her finger accusingly at Eve. "You ate the apple. The stranger from Earth has told us the story of how Eve ate the fruit on his planet. Satan tempted you. You're the one who ate the fruit, and then you gave it to your husband, and he ate it as well. Just like they did on Earth. Now, you're lying and trying to hide your horrible sin. The stranger may have even helped you to do it."

Eve kept her quiet demeanor. She looked at everyone with love in her heart. She waited for the crowd to calm. "I only met Adam, the man from Earth, a few times."

"You lie!" Zelbe said. "I saw you running and holding hands with the stranger. You were in love with him."

"You're the one who is lying," Adam retorted angrily. "Every word that comes out of your mouth is a lie. My wife has never been alone with the man from Earth. She has shown him nothing but kindness. We've all welcomed him here on Adon. He would not have caused us to eat the fruit. He knows what happened on his planet. He would never want that to happen here."

"You're just protecting your wife," Zelbe screamed at the top of her lungs so she could be heard over the murmuring crowd.

Someone whispered something in Zelba's ear, and she paused to listen.

"We have a witness who has come forward," she proclaimed. "There's a man here who says he saw Adam and Eve coming out of the garden that very night."

The man came forward and related his story.

Eve spoke, "We were in the garden that night as we are almost every night. God was there and we communed with him. Then we left. We didn't eat the fruit. Everything was normal when we left. We went home and went to sleep."

"Did you see us eat the fruit?" Adam asked the man.

The man shook his head no.

The crowd began talking loudly among themselves.

Elias raised his hand to silence the crowd. "See, this proves nothing. He saw Adam and Eve come out of the garden which they have freely admitted. All of you have seen them come out of the garden almost every night for many years."

"They lie. They ate the fruit, and now you are covering for them. They must die," Zelbe said.

Some in the crowd roared in approval. Most supported Adam and Eve.

Eve motioned for silence.

The crowd became so quiet Eve could almost hear her heart beating.

"We must show grace and mercy to whoever did this." Her words were spoken so sweetly, the crowd had to be quiet or they wouldn't have heard her. Eve's beauty radiated as she spoke. She was so beloved by everyone; her words were resonating.

"It wasn't my husband or I who ate the fruit. Someone did. We have to deal with it. But let's not become like Earth. Let's not let it destroy us. Let's not turn on each other. We've lived together and loved one another for all these years. God will forgive us if we will forgive each other."

"We will not stand by and let you kill someone and do something even more evil." Elias spoke forcefully for the first time in his life. None of them had ever spoken to each other this way before.

Eve tried one more time to calm everyone. "I have spoken to God," Eve said. "He has told me that there is a coming Messiah who will save us from our sins."

"The garden is destroyed," Zelbe interrupted Eve and said with a growl. "God said that whoever ate of the fruit had to die. God will not forgive us. You must die."

Eve tried to speak but was drowned out by the crowd.

"Let's draw lots," Zelbe said. "If the lots show that you did it, then you must die."

Some in the crowd roared in approval. A man brought Zelbe two blades of grass.

Zelbe said, "Adam, come and pull one of the blades of grass. If it's the long blade, then you're the one who ate the apple. If it's the short blade, then you can go free."

Adam refused. "I'll not be a party to your folly. I didn't eat the fruit. You're wrong. Who made you judge and jury over us anyway?"

Zelbe pulled another man out of the crowd and forced him to pull a blade from her hand.

Satan made sure he pulled the long piece of grass.

"See, God has shown us who's guilty," Zelbe proclaimed. "God said that anyone who ate of the fruit must die. Adam and Eve ate the fruit and have brought God's wrath on us. They must die."

At that moment, Aza rushed onto the platform and seized Adam. Elias turned and saw Aza coming but reacted too late.

Aza plunged his knife into Adam's side. Blood gushed from the wound as Adam collapsed onto the stage.

Eve screamed and rushed to her husband's side. She lifted him and sat his head on her lap. Her hand had blood on it.

What does this mean? Is he going to die?

"Don't die my love," Eve said. "Stay with me. I love you so much. Surely you won't die."

Eve stroked his hair as another man plunged a sword into her back.

The crowd gasped as several turned their heads away at the horrible sight.

The sword pierced all the way through, the tip coming out slightly on her front side.

He pulled the sword back out as blood gushed from the wound.

How can this be? What is happening? Her body shook momentarily, and then she fell to the ground, releasing her hold on Adam's head.

Screams... Crying.

Some fled.

Mothers held their children, shielding their eyes.

Adam and Eve were dying on the platform. Elias and a group of men stood over them, protecting them from Aza and his men.

Zelbe quickly backed away from the crowd, cowering in fear. Aza and his men raised their weapons as a warning for everyone to stay away from them.

Adam was still alive.

He reached for Eve, barely finding the strength to sit up. He took his wife's hand as she lifted her head slightly to look toward him. He said her name. Eve slowly lifted her hand toward his face. "I'm still here, my love."

Adam spoke to Eve softly, weakly, "For six thousand years, you have been everything and more than I could ever want in a wife. I have loved you with all my heart. God blessed me when he gave you to me."

Eve tried to speak but could only form the words, "I love you."

With one final look, their eyes met, then they closed, and they breathed their last breaths.

As the crowd stood in stunned silence, Elias wept.

* * *

As soon as Adam heard the news that Adam and Eve were in danger, he ran from the spacecraft to where the crowd had gathered. He arrived as Adam slumped down onto Eve's body and rushed to the stage.

Two women were already slowly separating Adam and Eve's bodies from their last embrace. Adam took them both in his arms and wept bitterly, rocking back and forth.

A voice thundered from heaven. "What have you done? Where are Adam and Eve?"

Everyone stepped away from the platform except Adam who kept holding them.

God said to all the people, "Listen! Their blood cries out to me. It was not Adam and Eve who ate the fruit. They have worshiped me and served me all their lives. Because they were wrongly accused, and you have done this horrible thing, you are all under a curse. I will no longer provide food for you. When you work the ground, you will toil. When you give birth, I will make your pain severe. All the women will serve their husbands, and the men will eat food from the sweat of their brow. The serpent will crawl on his belly, and his head will be crushed."

God said to Aza, "You have shed innocent blood. You will be a restless wanderer on Adon. I will drive you into the desert away from my presence."

Aza cried out to God, "My punishment is more than I can bear. Whoever finds me will kill me. I have brought these curses on myself and our people."

But the Lord said, "Anyone who kills Aza will suffer vengeance seven times over." The Lord put a mark on Aza so no one who found him would kill him.

Aza left the Lord's presence and ran away. He took his family with him, and they settled somewhere in the east.

God then said in a loud voice, "You shall not touch the man from Earth. I have sent him here. Anyone who touches him will die."

God continued. "I will no longer clothe you with my glory."

Immediately, they realized they were all naked and ashamed and were trying to cover themselves. They all ran away to their houses to hide.

With those last words came silence.

Everyone was gone. God was gone.

Adam still held Adam and Eve's lifeless bodies. A butterfly came and lit on Eve's head.

The entire creation mourned her death.

* * *

Later that night, Adam lay in his bed unable to sleep, the shame of his actions haunted him. He could hear the screams and could still see the look on Eve's face as the color drained and life left her. She still had a look of elegance, of peace, even in death.

He couldn't fathom that he'd caused all this pain. He felt like the sin of the world was on his shoulders. Adam and Eve were dead because of him. The garden no longer existed because of him.

I wish I had never come to this planet. If I hadn't, Eve would still be alive.

At that moment, a bright light filled his spacecraft. Night had fallen, and darkness had filled the night sky. Adam rushed to the observation tower. He looked out at the dazzling display of splendor dominating the sky.

The brightest star he'd ever seen was rising in the east.

THE EDEN STORIES

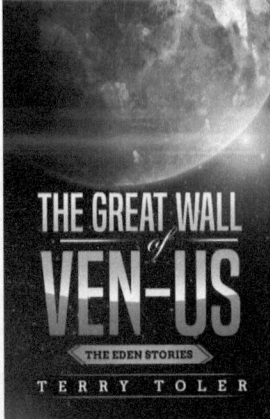

About the Author

TERRY TOLER is the author of the Jamie Austen and Alex Halee book series along with *The Eden Stories*. He is a minister, public speaker, counselor, and retired entrepreneur. Impacting the lives of people worldwide through storytelling has become one of his passions in life. He can be followed at terrytoler.com.